Two Man Advantage

Hat Trick Book Two

Samantha Wayland

Two Man Advantage

Copyright © 2013 Samantha Wayland

Published by Loch Awe Press
P.O. Box 5481
Wayland, MA 01778

ISBN 9781940839035

Edited by Helen Hardt and Meghan Conrad
Cover Art by Caitlin Fry

Also by Samantha Wayland

Destiny Calls
With Grace
Hat Trick Book One: Fair Play
Hat Trick Book Three: End Game

Dedication

For Victoria Morgan—coach, therapist, artist, author, and most importantly, dear friend. Thank you.

Acknowledgements

As always, I must thank my beloved husband, who does everything in his power to see I have the time, space, energy and quiet needed to write my stories.

Many thanks also to Victoria Morgan, Penny Watson, Bobbi Ruggiero and Stephanie Kay for their support and friendship. Thanks to Dalton Diaz for *still* being my rock. And to Serena Bell, who makes me think harder and write better.

To my friend Meghan Conrad (www.meghanconrad.com), for her patience and humor. I can't imagine looking forward to edits more than I look forward to hers. I don't always take her advice (no, his voice did *not* sound like bananas moving over velvet, whatever the hell that means) but there is no doubt my stories wouldn't be the same without her valuable input. Also, she's awesome and super pretty.

Chapter One

Garrick bolted upright in bed. "I'm sorry. Can you please repeat that slowly? Because I'm abso-fucking-lutely certain I heard you wrong."

Savannah's husky laugh buzzed down the phone line. If Garrick's mouth hadn't been gaping open with shock, he'd have smiled at the sinful delight in her chuckle.

"You heard me just fine, Garrick."

That might be true, but he still couldn't make sense of it. They were in the midst of their nightly phone call, a practice they'd started since Savannah had left for Boston a few weeks before—leaving him several hundred miles away in Moncton, New Brunswick. As often happened, the conversation had turned to sex. Phone sex.

It wasn't the same as the real thing. *At all*. But it was all they had until he could move to Boston.

Garrick swallowed. "I'm pretty sure you just suggested I should go find a boyfriend."

"Hmm..." Savannah purred thoughtfully. "Maybe not a *boyfriend*."

"I should think not."

"But a lover. A *male* lover."

He was speechless.

"Garrick?"

"*Really?*"

She laughed. "Yes, really."

He didn't know what to say. He still wasn't sure he understood. "But I'm in love with *you*."

"I know. But you're horny, and you haven't been with a man in over a decade, and well..."

He gripped the phone tighter, afraid of what might come

next.

"...I thought it would be hot. You know. Because then you could tell me about it."

Now he laughed. She had a serious kink for hearing about his past exploits with men. But those were in the past. Savannah was his future. Unless...

"Does this mean things have changed? That you don't want..." He couldn't finish the question, trying and utterly failing to sound neutral.

"No."

Relief loosened his death grip on the phone. "Okay, so this is just..."

"Fun. I hope. Or that was the idea."

"Oh."

Savannah sighed. "Garrick, I love you. I trust you. I know we're together. But I don't believe absolute monogamy is required."

He chuckled. "You've been reading Dan Savage again, haven't you?"

"Listening to the podcasts, actually. But yes, and I think he's right. We're committed to each other and I want to you have what you want. What you need."

"But what about you? My needs don't trump yours."

"You'll be meeting both our needs. Look, you like having sex with men. And I *really* like hearing about it. It's not more complicated than that. Or I don't mean for it to be. Phone sex is great for me. And I have this veritable treasure trove of battery-powered goodies you shipped me off to the States with. I'm more than content. You're not."

"I am," he said quickly. And it was true. Of course—*hell yes*—he'd be happier in Boston with her, but they had a few months to go before he could make the move. In the meantime, jacking off, even during phone sex with Savannah, was definitely not doing more than taking the edge off.

"You're not, Garrick. I know you'd never cheat and you'd

willingly live like a monk until we're together again. But I want you to be more than content. I want you to have fun. I want you to be happy."

"I *am* happy."

Savannah growled. "Are you being purposely obtuse or does the idea really repulse you?"

He smiled. "I'm being *unintentionally* obtuse, if that's possible." He lay back on his bed, relaxing into the pillows for the first time since Savannah had dropped her bomb. "And I'm still not sure what to say."

"Say you'll think about it. And then promise you won't agree unless you're sure. I don't mean to pressure you into anything. It was just...an idea, I guess."

"No," he said. "I mean, no, don't feel bad. It's an interesting idea."

"Interesting?" she asked, a hint of a smile in her voice.

He rubbed a hand over his naked belly and stretched out his legs, letting them fall open. "Yeah, interesting."

"Think about it, Garrick. A man. Remember how it was with David? How different it felt? How much stronger, bigger, *thicker* your lover would feel?"

He hummed and closed his eyes. Savannah was shamelessly pushing all his buttons.

God, he loved her.

"You're thinking about it, aren't you?" she asked.

"I am," he admitted. He wrapped his hand around his growing erection. His blood flowed thick and hot, his body flushing warm.

"Do you have someone in mind?"

An image, a face, popped into his mind. He squashed it. That was madness. "No. Maybe."

Savannah laughed. "You don't have to tell me now. I can wait."

God, *he* couldn't. He bent his knees, spreading them. His

hand took on a steady rhythm.

"But you do have to tell me," she said. "Everything. In detail."

Garrick groaned and rubbed his palm over the head of his erection. She was killing him.

"Now, where were we?" she murmured, and with a moan, dragged them both back into the vividly detailed fantasy she'd been whispering in his ear not ten minutes before.

Only now, try as he might, his lover had a face.

Rhian dodged to the right, trying not to jostle the people packed around him in the crowded bar. He wasn't big on being touched in any circumstances, but if Deena succeeding in touching his face, he might have to go home and shower.

Everyone knew Deena was working her way through the team. Any player witless enough to be with her ended up as nothing more than another notch on her bedpost. She'd worked hard to earn her puck bunny status and appeared to revel in it. Rhian couldn't imagine why anyone would be proud of such a thing. He was all for the occasional *discreet* casual encounter, but he wasn't the least bit interested in helping Deena further her goal or her reputation.

When she leaned in again, he grabbed her wrist.

"Ree-in, what's wrong?"

Rhian sighed. "It's Rhian."

"What?"

"My name is *Rhian*. Pronounced RYE-in. Like Nolan Ryan?"

"Who?"

"Ryan O'Neal?"

"What are you talking about?"

"Ryan Seacrest?"

"Oh! I get it!"

No, she really didn't. Why the fuck had he come here tonight?

Deena tugged against his grip, but he didn't let go until he was sure she wouldn't try to molest him again. She rubbed her wrist as if he'd hurt her, gazing up at him with a pathetic, wounded expression.

He tried very hard not to let his revulsion show.

"Please don't touch me." His words were polite—the tone, not so much.

Deena's gaze narrowed, and if anything, she looked even more determined.

God help me. Figuring divine intervention was a long shot, he searched the bar for help. He found Dave Chambers and Chris Kimball in one corner, flirting with a couple of women he'd never seen before, while Tim Robineau bickered at the bar with the latest in a long and painful line of poorly chosen girlfriends. In other words, *situation normal.*

Rhian used to count on Garrick to run interference on the rare occasion this sort of shit happened, but Garrick had all but disappeared since Savannah had moved to Boston. It didn't seem like Garrick's style to mope, but the man had been MIA for weeks, except at the gym and on the ice.

Then again, what the hell did Rhian know about being in love?

He was about to give up on finding a wingman, when he spotted a familiar face in the crowd. He did a double-take. A man was working his way through the crush of bodies. He smiled and waved when he caught Rhian's gaze.

"Rhian! Hi!"

"Steve?" Rhian barely checked the instinct to back away.

"Yeah, hey. How are you?"

"I'm...uh...I'm great. Wow. What are you doing here?"

Rhian wasn't just asking for kicks. He'd last seen Steve in Chicago, what felt like a lifetime ago. A lifetime Rhian had cheerfully left behind.

Deena watched their exchange with great interest, eyeing Steve like he was a hunk of filet mignon and she'd been dining on nothing but Kraft dinner for a month.

"I came to see you, buddy!" Steve cried, as if *of course,* and wasn't this great news?

Rhian blinked. "You did?"

"Sure!" Steve turned to smile at Deena. "And who is this lovely creature?"

She stepped closer to Steve. "I'm Deena," she said, her voice far huskier than it had been not thirty seconds before.

"Steve." He took her hand and didn't let go.

If Deena's slow smile and adoring gaze was anything to go by, she was charmed. "And how do you know Rhian?"

At least she got my name right this time, he thought sourly.

"I'm his brother," Steve said.

Rhian's jaw almost hit the floor. "You are *not* my brother."

Steve stuck his chin out. "We're *family.*"

"I have no family." The bald truth was out of his mouth before he had time to consider the wisdom of airing his dirty laundry to Deena or anyone else. Christ, he was surrounded by teammates, fans, and friends.

Deena's eyebrows climbed way up as she looked back and forth between them, eventually settling on Steve. "You'll have to excuse him. He was in a nasty mood before you arrived."

Rhian wrestled with his burning desire to flee and slapped on a bright smile. "Deena, why don't we go to the bar and get another round?"

She shot him a wide-eyed, disbelieving look. He couldn't blame her. Still smiling, he moved to take her elbow, but Steve stepped between them.

"No, please, allow me," he offered, settling his hand on the small of her back. "Unless Rhian has any objection?"

Deena shot Rhian a scathing glare and looped her arm through Steve's. "Hardly," she drawled. "And it wouldn't matter if he did."

Steve turned back to Rhian with a wide grin. "See you

around, bud?"

Not if I see you first.

Rhian managed to nod once.

As soon as Deena turned away, Steve winked and mouthed the words "you're welcome."

Rhian's guts churned as Deena and Steve fought their way to the bar through the crush of people. Steve showing up out of nowhere couldn't be anything but trouble. The guy was a shit-storm magnet. Hell, it had to be a miracle he wasn't in prison by now. When they'd parted ways at age eighteen, Steve had seemed bound and determined to join his old man in the Illinois State Penitentiary.

Maybe Steve had just been released? Which would mean he probably shouldn't be in Canada. Either way, Rhian wanted nothing to do with any of it.

The bright chirp of Deena's voice carried over the rumble of the crowd and the music pumping from the speakers. She appeared to be having a great time. She was an adult. There was little Rhian could do, in any case.

This night had started poorly and gone steadily downhill since.

Rhian grabbed his coat and left.

Chapter Two

Garrick sat at the desk in his study and stared balefully at the mountains of paperwork surrounding him.

How the fuck was he going to keep up with all of this?

In a few short weeks, he would be part-owner of the Moncton Ice Cats. He had spent the last twelve years playing for his hometown's EHL hockey team, but that would all change when the league approved the deal put forward by him, two of Savannah's brothers—both NHL players—and the previous owner, the notoriously reclusive, Edwin "Reese" Lamont. Until then, the identity of the stakeholders in their new corporation—except Lamont—was being kept secret, so on the remote chance the deal fell through, they could walk away without anyone being the wiser.

In the meantime, Garrick was trapped in a delicate and uncomfortable game of balancing his responsibilities as a forward on the ice and a paper-pushing desk jockey off it.

For years he'd dreaded what would become of his life once he left the ice. Now he was practically counting the minutes. He'd already convinced their coach, Rick, to bump him out of the first line. The result wasn't a lot less playing time or responsibility to the team, but it took off some of the pressure. Sort of.

Yeah, no pressure at all.

He surveyed the piles of folders and randomly grabbed one.

Reese's personal assistant was a compulsive organizer. Everything she sent over was in a color coded folder. Inside these, there were often a host of sticky flags of various colors to indicate a litany of things Garrick was meant to review, act on, read about, or god only knew what. Because really, what was the point of this maniacal system if no one bothered to explain it to him? *None.*

He flipped open the plain manila folder. It wasn't one of the countless documents sent over by Reese, but one that Mark, the team's departing manager, had passed off. It was the team roster, along with recommendations on what to do about that roster.

Garrick slapped the folder closed and shoved it in a drawer.

He'd been looking forward to being an owner and helping to craft a new team from the Ice Cats' already-solid foundation. He'd somehow blithely ignored that he would be on point to make decisions that would make and break people's careers. And that some of those people would be his friends.

He picked up the next folder and was relieved to find nothing more controversial than the bids for the proposed construction at the arena. First, some remodeling for the game-time vendors. Then later, over the summer, serious changes to the rink itself, including the ability to lay down parquet to host basketball games and other events.

He scanned the endless columns of numbers until his vision blurred and he stopped to rub his eyes. Christ, he needed sleep. He tilted back in his chair and his eyes immediately slid shut. He'd been up late every night for the past two weeks attempting to get on top of this pile. Maybe it was time to admit defeat, get some rest, and make a fresh run at it tomorrow.

He was just about to give in to the fantasy of going to bed early when the phone rang. He reached for it without opening his eyes.

"LeBlanc."

"Garrick! Hello. Did I catch you at a good time?" There was no need for the caller to identify himself. Anyone who knew Rupert Smythe would recognize his very proper British accent.

"Hey, Rupert. What's up?"

"Yes, well, I wanted to speak with you about something. If you have a moment."

Garrick's eyes snapped open and his feet returned to the

floor with a thump. Rupert only sounded this uptight and excruciatingly polite when he was upset or about to share bad news. Garrick rubbed his eyes. He shouldn't have answered the damn phone.

"What's up?"

"I have a bit of a family situation. A brother gone missing."

Garrick hadn't known Rupert had a brother. "Couldn't he be on vacation or something? Run off with some woman?"

"He's four."

"Ah." Rupert had to be a few years into his thirties, but Garrick kept the obvious—and nosey—questions to himself.

"As you can imagine, I'm a bit concerned. I need to see if I can find him and his mother."

"Sure. Of course."

He could appreciate Rupert's situation, but he didn't like where this was going. Rupert was due in Moncton this week to take on the role of the Ice Cats' manager.

"I'm sure it's just a mix up and I'll find them in a matter of days, but I'm going to have to fly back to London to start. My best guess is I won't be in Moncton for another week or two. I can do the job from abroad, mostly, but obviously, it won't be the same as being there."

"But Mark's last day is this week." Garrick snapped his mouth shut, horrified at how close he'd come to whining.

"Yes, I know. I'll call and ask if he can stick it out."

Mark was already arriving at his new job a week later than they wanted. No way in hell he was going to stick anything out—least of all his neck—when his new employers were waiting.

Garrick sighed. He was a fucking idiot, but he made the offer anyway. "I'll cover for you where I can, but you're going to have to call in all the decisions."

"Yes, of course."

Mark was the only one associated with the team who knew

the identities of the new owners. Garrick had been more or less managing the team alongside Mark for the better part of two weeks while Mark packed up his life and got ready to move. What would a couple more weeks do?

Except maybe kill him from exhaustion.

For some reason, Savannah's suggestion that he take a lover popped into his head. He almost laughed out loud. He'd have to schedule *gay sex* right between *showering* and *paperwork*.

Who was he kidding?

Half his mind already on the tasks before him, his dream of going to bed crushed, he muttered a few more reassurances to Rupert and said goodnight.

He'd barely dug into the bids when a car horn sounded from out front.

Jesus. *Welcome to Grand Central Station*. Didn't anyone fucking sleep anymore? He was never going to get shit done with all these distractions.

He stood and stretched. The only consolation was that, in this case, he was happy to have company for his misery. He'd recognized the signature three-blast greeting and this would be just the man for the job.

He opened his front door and waved to Jack Chevalier as he hopped out of his truck. He and Jack had grown up together, and he was Garrick's oldest friend.

"Evening," Jack called as he mounted the porch stairs two at a time.

Must be nice to have that kind of energy. "Hey, you're just the person I need."

"I am?" Jack asked, hesitating at the threshold.

Garrick stood back and gestured him into the house. "Yeah, I was reviewing the construction bids."

Jack stood awkwardly in the small front hall, noticeably *not* taking off his coat. "Actually, that's what I wanted to talk to you about."

Garrick knew that tone of voice. "No."

"No?"

"No, Jack. To whatever you're going to say, no. No, you can't quit. No, you're not the wrong man for the job. No, you're not missing a single qualification we need. No, none of the other partners are worried about it either."

Jack's lips twitched. "I can't decide if it's flattering or frightening that you knew what I was going to say."

Garrick didn't have to be a genius to figure it out, since they'd already been over this three times in the last two weeks alone.

"Jack, you're the perfect project manager. We need someone we can trust, who knows the city and the players in it, and who has experience in food service and construction."

"And an inexperienced ex-con with no formal education is it, huh?"

Garrick resisted the temptation to smack his friend in the back of the head. "You have the experience. You worked for your old man's construction company for years."

"When I was a teenager."

"And you've taken classes in hotel and restaurant management."

"In prison."

"And I'd trust you with my life."

At least Jack had no argument for that. Garrick waited, not taking a real breath until Jack peeled off his coat and tossed it on the bench.

"Okay, it's your money."

Garrick grunted. "I'm not worried."

He led the way to his kitchen to make coffee. Jack stood back and watched him.

"You look tired," Jack said.

"Thanks, Mom."

Jack grinned, his blue eyes sparkling. For the first time in years, Garrick was struck by how handsome he was. Savannah had given Garrick a ration of shit for not warning her before she met Jack that he was, in her words, *that gorgeous*. When he smiled like that, Garrick could see what she meant.

He thought about Savannah's offer again. It had been a long, long time since he and Jack had talked about sex. Long enough ago that it had been the bragging of young men who didn't know better. Now it occurred to Garrick that he hadn't seen Jack with a woman—or a man—since he'd regained his freedom.

Jack cocked his head and looked at him oddly. Garrick realized he'd been staring.

Goddamn Savannah. She was going to be the death of him.

Turning back to the coffee, he considered whether he could be with Jack. He immediately discarded the idea. Jack *was* beautiful. And a great guy. A good friend. But he was like a brother to Garrick, and thinking about him that way was kind of creepy.

Another man's face popped into his head again and he slammed the kettle back on the stove with a thunk.

What was the matter with him? Savannah suggested he take a lover and ever since he couldn't stop picturing the straightest arrow he'd ever met.

Idiot.

Rhian yanked his duffel from the closet and tossed it on his bed. The Ice Cats were hitting the road tomorrow and he needed to pack.

Seven minutes later, he dropped the bag by his front door and wondered what the hell he was going to do with the rest of his night. Looking around the apartment, he frowned at the butt-ugly furniture and artwork. He'd rented the place furnished, and the only thing he'd added was the huge LCD TV in the living room. It was the first and only thing he'd ever purchased that wasn't either a necessity, something to further his hockey career, or that kept him safe.

Collapsing on the couch, he turned on his pride and joy and began a vigorous channel-surfing session. He couldn't find a damn thing he wanted to watch tonight, but he kept going.

Seeing Steve had unsettled him, which was ridiculous and infuriating. Steve had no hold over him. Hell, they were practically strangers. They hadn't laid eyes on each other in years, and contrary to Steve's assertion, being in the same foster home for a few months did *not* make them anything like family.

Maybe that was it. The "brothers" thing had really thrown Rhian for a loop. What was that shit? Totally bizarre.

He paused in his rush through the channels when a lot of naked skin popped up on the screen. A woman pretended to be in ecstasy while she rode some guy in a reverse cowgirl position.

Rhian's dick twitched—more like reflex than any real interest—before he moved on to the next channel.

Maybe that was his problem? Normally, he'd indulge in the occasional hook up to take the edge off, but he hadn't in months.

And he definitely had an edge to grind tonight.

He would go out while they were on the road, he decided, trying to psyche himself up. He could find a woman interested in a little fun, and together they could achieve some mutual satisfaction.

And wow, *that* idea left him totally cold. His dick didn't even bother with the reflexive twitch this time.

What was the matter with him? For some reason, these days he'd rather hang out with his friends than get laid. Which was weird. Dry spells were hardly unheard of, but the hanging out with friends thing? That was new for Rhian.

In fact, Garrick was the nearest thing to a close friend Rhian had ever had, and he had no idea how it had happened. He'd arrived in Moncton a year ago, content to do his usual thing—keep to himself, play hard, move on and hopefully, up. Then Garrick had sucked him in and before he knew what had hit him, it was beers out with the team, watching football games, and poker night at Garrick's place.

Next thing he knew, he was one of the guys. And enjoying the hell out of it, too.

Except for nights like tonight, when he was forced to admit friends were a lot like *roots*, and Rhian didn't do roots. He knew better.

No attachments. No entanglements.

Now it would be hard to leave when the time came. Well, maybe not *hard*, but not as easy as it should have been.

Rhian could pack up his entire life, including the stupid TV, in ninety minutes. Two hours, max, and he'd be ready to move. It was best to be prepared. Ready to bug out. Follow the hockey, the money, the safety.

He had no knick-knacks, no childhood trophies—though he'd earned plenty, they'd all been stolen, destroyed, or tossed out—nothing to slow him down.

Until now. Now he'd have to say goodbye to his friends. He'd have to figure out a way to stay in touch, at least with Garrick. And that was different. So different, he still wasn't sure how he felt about it.

He hadn't realized how much had changed until Garrick had stopped showing up at all the shit he used to drag Rhian to. Now, Rhian wanted to go out and have a beer, he wanted to spend time with people—with *Garrick*. But his friend, the heart of their group, the reason Rhian was suddenly all fucked up about this shit, had disappeared.

Fucking Garrick. Bad enough the guy was so in love with Savannah he practically walked around with stars in his eyes, now he was blowing off his friends so he could go home and moon over her?

Not that Rhian didn't like Savannah. He did. Hell, he could even understand why a man might moon over her, too. She was gorgeous, sexy, smart, and on the short list of people Rhian now thought of as a friend. He'd even hit on her once, but she'd shot him down. That Garrick had worked his way past her considerable defenses was something of a miracle.

Even more miraculous was that Rhian missed her. Another new thing. Missing someone.

Rhian shook his head. He knew better. No attachments. No things. At any moment he could move to a new apartment, a new city.

For the first time in his life, the promise of another fresh start sounded less shiny and fresh, and more...lonely.

Chapter Three

Rhian chucked his duffel into the luggage compartment under the team bus and went to the door. Before he could climb aboard, though, movement in the parking lot caught his eye.

Apologizing to the guys behind him, he stepped out of line. Deena's eyes widened when she saw him coming toward her, but she stood her ground, her chin tilted at a defiant angle.

The dead-eyed stare and attitude were completely undermined by her badly swollen, blackened right eye.

Rhian felt sick. "Are you okay?"

She laughed, the sound strident in the cold morning air. "I'm fine."

"Did Steve—"

"That's none of your business," she snapped.

She was right, of course. He forced himself to respect that, even while he hated it. If he saw Steve again Rhian would ask him, and regardless of the asshole's answer, try to convince him to go the fuck away.

"You should have it looked at," he offered lamely. He wished Savannah were still the team's trainer. She'd have jumped in and not made either of them feel stupid.

"Fuck you."

Or maybe not.

He sighed. "Look, I'm sorry. I never thought—"

Deena laughed again. "Relax, Rhee-Ann. Some girls like it rough. If you ever got laid, maybe you'd know that."

He didn't rise to the bait. He'd been here before, with Steve, with other kids in the homes. "If you need help, you can come to me."

Deena rolled her eyes. "Did you hear a word I said?"

He had. He'd heard all the things she hadn't said, too. And he'd known she wouldn't thank him. That wasn't why he'd offered. "I just wanted you to know."

"Yeah, well, I'm all set."

Rhian shrugged. "Offer stands."

He caught another eye roll as he turned away. He ignored it. The creeping dread wasn't as easy to shake off. This was his old life. The one he'd worked so hard to leave behind. The one he'd sworn he'd never go back to. Now his past was a black smudge polluting his time in Moncton.

Goddamn Steve. Goddamn Deena for not kicking Steve in the nuts and walking away. For not accepting help.

Head down, fists jammed into his coat pockets, he got back into line to get on the bus.

A shoulder bumped into his. "Hey, Rhi."

Rhian looked up at Garrick. He couldn't imagine what his friend saw on his face. Frustration. Anger. Maybe shock that the simple gesture from a good friend could make him feel better. Whatever it was, Garrick's hand landed on his shoulder and gripped tightly.

"You okay?" Garrick asked. He glanced over Rhian's shoulder and his eyes widened. He'd obviously spotted Deena.

"Yeah, I'm fine."

Garrick searched his face. Rhian really didn't want to get into it now, but he also didn't want Garrick to think he had anything to do with that black eye. "I left her at the bar last night with someone I used to know," he said by way of explanation.

Garrick frowned and glanced at Deena. "I'm assuming she didn't look like that when you did."

Rhian sighed. "No. I never thought...I wouldn't...."

"Of course." Garrick squeezed his shoulder again.

It was their turn to get on the bus. Garrick let go of his shoulder and Rhian felt like he'd been cut loose from his mooring. More than just being pathetic, it rattled him that

Garrick's support mattered so much.

Moving on autopilot, he went to a window seat in the middle of the bus and looked back at Garrick. They didn't have assigned seating or anything, and they didn't always sit with the same guys, but he and Garrick sat together more often than not.

He was surprised when Garrick hesitated at the front of the bus where team management and the coaching staff usually sat. Rhian belatedly noticed the bulging leather bag overflowing with paperwork swinging from Garrick's shoulder.

Garrick glanced up at Rhian, his deep brown eyes telegraphing his concern. With a final glance at the empty front row, he moved farther along the aisle to the seat next to Rhian.

Rhian ignored the wave of relief and turned to make room for Garrick. He eyed his friend's briefcase. "You forget to pay your bills?" He quirked an eyebrow. "For the last six months?"

Garrick chuckled. "Something like that." He shoved the bag into the overhead compartment. "But it can wait until later."

Rhian wondered when that would be, since they were either at events, on the ice, or on the bus for most of the next three days. He didn't ask. Selfishly, he wanted Garrick to distract him. Just for a little while. Just long enough to leave Moncton behind for a couple days and pretend the black cloud of Steve's arrival might clear out while they were gone.

Garrick plunked down in the seat next to Rhian and scrubbed his hands over his face. He should be sitting up at the front of the bus getting work done, but he hadn't been able to resist sitting with his friends. With Rhian.

The thing with Deena sucked. He wanted to ask if he could do anything, but he figured he knew the answer. He couldn't remember Rhian ever being as upset. Rhian generally kept whatever he was feeling or thinking to himself. Hell, it had taken months after his arrival in Moncton for Rhian to relax enough to talk about anything other than hockey.

In fact, almost a year later, Garrick still knew very little about Rhian. His comment about seeing someone he used to know made Garrick realize he'd never met anyone from Rhian's life. No friends. Family. Former teammates. No one.

He studied his friend, who stood with one knee on the cushion, twisted toward Garrick as he spoke over their seats to the guys sitting behind them.

Garrick's nose was right at the height of Rhian's cock. His brain went sideways. Not that he could see anything behind the denim pulled tight across Rhian's hips, but Garrick had an excellent imagination. And even without that, he had a keen appreciation for that tight belly and those lean hips. If he closed his eyes, he could picture them perfectly, regardless of how studiously he'd tried not to notice any such thing in the locker room.

Garrick was fit. Most of the team was somewhere between beefy and buff. Rhian, though, was *ripped*. There wasn't an ounce of fat on him. Garrick knew. He'd looked and looked and never found a one.

Rhian's devotion to the game extended far beyond the ice. He pushed himself in the gym harder than anyone. When Savannah had been the trainer, she'd had to modify Rhian's workout routine several times to keep up with his achievements. A lot of the guys were in awe of Rhian, Garrick among them. Though Garrick was likely the only one who couldn't get over Rhian's ass being *that* tight and round.

Rhian dropped into his seat and Garrick snapped his eyes forward. He probably shouldn't just sit there and ogle his friend's junk. Wouldn't want anyone to get the wrong impression.

Or the right one.

"Hey, you all right?" Rhian asked.

Garrick smiled, keeping his eyes firmly above Rhian's neck. "That was going to be my question."

Rhian's smile faded. "Yeah, I'm fine. But I'm not the one I'm worried about."

Garrick nodded, wishing he had some comfort to offer.

Soon they were surrounded by their teammates and the bus was pulling out of the parking lot. It was easy to fall into the old routine. He talked to his friends, ribbing Tim about his girlfriends, railing on Chris for his perpetual lack thereof, listening to stories about everyone's families. For twelve years, this had been Garrick's life. Something he'd enjoyed and looked forward to. Now it was different.

None of them knew about Savannah except Rhian. And not even Rhian knew Garrick wasn't just one of the guys anymore. Not just another player on the team. Soon, he would be their boss.

He was an imposter, surrounded by people who thought he was their friend.

Tim and Dave started giving Garrick shit about his recent disappearance and monastic—as far as they knew—lifestyle. He laughed, firing back across the aisle, before turning to Rhian, the only person who knew why he was off the market. Rhian's grin lit up his face, his dark blue eyes dancing with their shared secret.

Garrick couldn't look away. He hoped like hell his face didn't show any of what he was thinking.

Rhian had the body of a god. And it was only fitting, since he had the face of an angel.

Full lips, long dark lashes tipped with gold to match his blond curls, and cobalt eyes accented by crow's feet radiating from the corners. Though not *real* crow's feet. Not like Garrick's, which had started to deepen in the past few years. Rhian's had likely always been there, a genetic blessing, since at the tender age of twenty-four, he hadn't gone enough miles to actually warrant wrinkles.

Unlike Garrick, who was practically old enough to be Rhian's *father*. Okay, maybe ten years wasn't quite sufficient an age gap for that, but right then it felt damn close. He'd never given Rhian's age a moment's thought in the past year. Not until now, when he couldn't seem to break their locked gazes. Now seemed like a good time to remember how young his friend was.

Garrick swallowed the drool pooling in his mouth and tried hard not to look like he wanted to grab the front of Rhian's shirt in both hands and haul him close enough to kiss.

What the hell had Savannah done to him?

Rhian finally blinked. His brows lowered. Garrick tore his eyes away and stared at the seat in front of him.

Shit.

Desperate for a diversion, he turned back to Tim across the aisle, who was offering to remedy Garrick's lack of love life by introducing him to some women.

Garrick tried to appear suitably appalled. "Dude, with your taste in women, I'd rather be celibate."

Hoots of laughter erupted around them and Garrick took a moment to collect himself while several of the guys offered their own obscene suggestions.

Rhian's thigh bumped his, their knees knocking. Garrick swallowed hard then turned toward his friend.

Rhian studied Garrick's face with a narrow gaze.

"What's up?" Garrick asked, trying to brazen out his misstep. For Christ's sake, he'd been ogling the most straight-laced guy he'd ever met. The good news was Rhian probably couldn't even compute a man looking at him like that for what it was.

He refused to pull his leg away from Rhian's. They'd probably sat like this a hundred times before. He just couldn't remember it. Maybe because until Savannah had filled his head with crazy ideas, it hadn't mattered.

It doesn't matter now, he reminded himself sternly.

After what felt like an eternity, Rhian shrugged and looked forward. "Nothing. Sorry."

Garrick didn't know what to make of that. Or that Rhian didn't join back into the conversation sailing over their seats.

Or pull his thigh away from Garrick's.

Garrick seriously regretted putting his bag in the overhead compartment. He could have used one of those folders on his lap right about now. Instead, he shoved his hands in his coat pockets and tugged the leather down over his hips—and the erection he couldn't control to save his life.

If Rhian wanted to sit and stare out the window at nothing, that was fine with Garrick. He could use a few minutes to himself.

Tipping his head back, he closed his eyes, intending to rest them for just a moment. They weren't a mile outside Moncton before he passed out.

Chapter Four

Rhian barely noticed the incredible views from the Confederation Bridge as the bus drove onto PEI. He'd spent most of the trip staring out the window. Now, while everyone else on the bus was doing just that, he gave in to what he'd wanted to be doing all along.

Staring at Garrick.

He'd fallen asleep not long after they'd gotten underway. He'd looked tired, but Rhian was surprised he was still out cold. Conversation had flowed around them the entire trip, people had bumped into his seat, and one section of the highway had been so badly pitted with potholes it had rattled Rhian's teeth. Garrick slept on.

He looked different this way and it took Rhian a while to figure out why. Then he laughed to himself. This was the first time he'd seen Garrick when he wasn't talking, laughing, or wearing his game face. For once he looked peaceful.

And as always, handsome.

Garrick's soft brown eyes were closed, and his big contagious smile was in hibernation, but the cheekbones, the soft curling hair at his collar, and the first strands of gray at the temple were familiar. Beautiful.

Rhian tore his gaze away, staring down at where his thigh ran the length of Garrick's, and sighed.

Once upon a time, he'd been more...*flexible* in his choice of lovers, but he'd put all that behind him once he'd started in the junior leagues. He'd had one ticket out of Chicago, and he hadn't been willing to do anything that would fuck it up. Having sex with men would have fucked it up. Could still fuck it up.

He had to stay focused on his goal. Hockey. The NHL. He had to keep his nose clean and his reputation sterling. Focus on the game.

Which was a damn shame, since when Garrick stared at him like he had earlier, Rhian wanted to fall to his knees and...well, there were any number of things he'd like to do once he got there. Starting with beg.

Garrick sat on the edge of his bed in another anonymous hotel room, this one in Charlottetown on Prince Edward Island, and stared at the mini-bar.

He'd spent the last hour going through a metric ton of paperwork, ending with the report from Mark. Now the contents of that folder were shoved back into his briefcase and he was determined to drink himself half-blind. They had to be at the rink early tomorrow morning and Garrick thought a pounding headache and roiling stomach at practice was the least punishment he deserved.

Fuck. He knew what he needed to do. He knew the right thing for the team was to trade away Justin Dubois—the *friend* he'd shared a locker room, laughter, and beers with for the past six years. But he couldn't do it, which made him feel like a failure *and* a coward.

Twisting open the nip of Jack Daniels, he threw it back with hardly a gasp of regret for his stomach lining.

He recalled the easy banter on the bus that morning. Justin had told a story about his five year old, Mandy, and how much she loved school. In Moncton. Where she'd lived her whole life. But then, maybe Mandy would grow to like Grand Forks, North Dakota. And maybe someday Uncle Garrick would forgive himself for sending her there or wherever the hell they ended up.

God, what had made him think he wanted to own a hockey team? Particularly *this* hockey team. *His* hockey team.

He was one stupid motherfucker.

The nip of Smirnoff went down with enough trouble that Garrick acknowledged, in hindsight, he should have used the twelve dollar bottle of orange juice to ease its way. He almost never drank hard alcohol and now he was getting a pretty clear memory of why.

He eyed the nip of Seagram's Gin and decided he wasn't suicidal. Gin made him crazy.

Two other nips, two tiny bottles of wine, one of champagne, and two mini cans of beer were all that was left in the fridge. When a man was six and a half feet tall and carrying around over two hundred and twenty pounds, that was not going to cut it.

Fortunately, the hotel had a bar.

The rest of the mini-bar's contents would make excellent night caps once the bartenders cut him off, so he slammed the fridge shut, scooped his room key from his desk, and headed out. He resisted giving the pile of folders the finger on his way past, as that would have lacked dignity.

Thirty seconds later he was in the lobby and making a beeline for the bar.

He would have made it, too, if he hadn't seen Rhian in a corner of the lobby, talking to another man. The conversation didn't appear friendly.

Changing course, Garrick put himself in Rhian's line of sight.

Rhian spotted Garrick hovering beyond the next cluster of chairs and couches and gave a tiny shake of his head. Garrick would understand. They'd communicated on the ice with far less.

Rhian returned his full focus to the man standing before him.

Steve.

"What the fuck are you doing here?" he asked, keeping his voice low.

"I came to see you play," Steve said, as if it were perfectly understandable.

"You drove all the way from Moncton to watch me play?" Rhian asked, incredulous.

"I came all the way from Chicago, man. That's why I'm up here freezing my nuts off."

In some alternate universe, Rhian would be flattered. But Rhian lived in reality. Unlike Steve, apparently. "Look, I don't know what you think is going on here, but—"

"Hey, man, don't get your panties in a bunch. I just came to hang out. We can party—"

"No," Rhian said vehemently. "We cannot party. There is no party."

"But—"

"I saw Deena."

Steve blinked and his face scrunched up. "So?"

Rhian clenched his hands into fists to keep them from wrapping around Steve's neck. "So what the fuck did you do, Steve?"

Steve's blank look gave Rhian pause. *Maybe it hadn't been Steve?*

"She had a black eye..." Rhian prompted, watching Steve's face closely to gauge his reaction.

"Oh, yeah. That." Steve waved his hand dismissively. "Whatever."

Years of practice at burying his emotions was the only reason Rhian could keep his anger in check. He stepped forward and shoved his face close to Steve's.

"Go home."

"What?"

"Go back to Chicago. Get the fuck out of here." Rhian couldn't possibly be any clearer. He met Steve's narrow gaze, glare for glare.

"You son of a bitch," Steve ground out. "You're going to keep it all for yourself, aren't you? You're too important to remember the rest of us?"

Important? The rest of who?

"Look, I don't know if you think I'm living a lavish lifestyle up here in the boonies and you can come up here and be some hanger-on, but this isn't the NHL," Rhian said through clenched teeth. He didn't bother to mention that he wouldn't be living that lifestyle even if it *was* the goddamn NHL.

"You'll get there soon," Steve said with absolute conviction.

Rhian wanted to laugh. Even he didn't have that much confidence, and it was *his* dream.

"And what? You'll be my entourage?"

The corner of Steve's mouth kicked up. "Hey, yeah. I like that."

Rhian ached to remove the smile from Steve's face with his fist. Instead he ground his teeth together until he could spit out his response. "No. Fucking. Way."

Steve's face turned red and contorted with rage. "Unbelievable," he said, his voice reduced to a rough whisper.

Rhian couldn't imagine which part of this bizarre scenario Steve found hard to believe. The whole fucking thing seemed preposterous to him.

He held perfectly still and waited for Steve's next move. It was as likely to be a tackle as a punch. Rhian hoped he could subdue Steve and get him out of the building before anyone started asking questions.

Then he remembered Garrick watching them and grimaced. There would already be questions. That alone had Rhian drawing himself up to his full height until he towered over Steve, their chests almost touching.

Steve retreated a step and Rhian followed, staring him down until Steve spun and stalked out of the hotel, his normally pale face and neck mottled crimson.

Rhian hoped the fucker kept going until he got all the way back to Illinois.

The moment the doors slid shut, Rhian looked at Garrick and nodded his thanks. He hadn't wanted the back-up, but he appreciated it. Garrick arched a single eyebrow, and Rhian shook his head, waving Garrick off with the hand he could barely uncurl from a fist.

Garrick held his gaze a moment longer, then turned and strode into the hotel bar.

Rhian collapsed into a chair and dropped his head into his hands. It took a few minutes to get steady. He'd give his right arm to go up to his room and shut out the world, but he couldn't.

He had to give Garrick some kind of explanation.

And he'd just sit here alone until he could come up with one.

Garrick couldn't decide what was worse—being dismissed by Rhian when the guy clearly could use a friend, or that the strange confrontation he'd witnessed in the lobby had completely sobered him up.

There was a cure for the second problem, at least, and he was going to get right on that.

Cutting a wide path around the familiar faces in the lounge, he stalked to the bar and planted his ass on a stool. He searched the rows of bottles behind the bartender until his eyes caught on the beer taps.

"Moosehead, please."

As the bartender moved away, the shadow of a smile drifted across Garrick's face. Moosehead was Savannah's favorite beer. That small, albeit tenuous, connection made him feel a little better.

So would drinking a lot of them, really fast.

He thanked the bartender and slugged back half the pint, trying to focus on his drink and not on the paperwork waiting for him upstairs. He kept his back to the room. Sitting with anyone on the team was only going to make it worse. He needed a distraction, damn it, not another reminder of that he was a complete asshole.

Movement in the mirror above the bar caught his eye and he looked at the reflection of the lobby behind him. Then he thought of Rhian. And Savannah's crazy offer.

Now *there* was a distraction.

And another reason to drink. In the blink of an eye, his first beer was gone, and he signaled to the bartender for a refill.

It had been a very long time since he'd considered being with a man, and while the attraction still simmered under the surface, years of strictly enforced self-programming had suppressed those desires quite effectively. Until now. Until Savannah had opened the Pandora's Box of his desires. Now he couldn't stop thinking about it. About *him.*

Garrick stared down at his beer and snorted, imagining telling his good friend and teammate that he wanted a piece of his ass. Actually, he wanted every glorious well-toned inch of it. Was there a worse fucking nightmare than how Rhian would react if Garrick propositioned him?

As if on cue, Rhian walked into the bar and made his way toward Garrick. *Perfect.*

Garrick wanted to laugh.

And smash his head on the bar.

Hard.

Chapter Five

Rhian strode toward Garrick, determined to offer a limited version of the truth about what had happened in the lobby then retreat to his room.

He smiled and said hi to the guys as he passed, not stopping until Alexei and Mike waved him over. He went to their table, telling himself he wasn't chickening out. Just delaying the inevitable a little.

Alexei Belov was the team's resident crazy Russian, a reputation he gleefully lived up to at any opportunity. His pranks and ridiculous jokes—coupled with a thick accent that rendered most of the punch lines almost indecipherable—were often at the expense of his teammates, but no one minded. He made them laugh and never picked on anyone who couldn't take the ribbing or fire back. That he was a damn fine goalie also meant he got a lot of latitude from management, even the time the locker room and all of its inhabitants had ended up covered in shaving cream and BENGAY.

Alexei's best friend, Mike Erdo, sat next to him. A defenseman like Rhian, he was Alexei's polar opposite. Diplomatic where Alexei was brash. Gentle where his friend was more like the proverbial bull in a china shop.

Other than Garrick, Rhian spent the most time with these two. Standing at their table, one eye on Garrick to make sure he didn't go anywhere, Rhian realized he would miss them, too, when the time came to move on.

Given that Rhian had zero experience with this kind of shit, he hadn't the foggiest idea how he would go about telling either of them that he wanted to stay in touch. Stay friends. Not that he was going anywhere right then, but eventually...

He glanced back at the bar—again. Garrick was slumped on his stool, looking more dejected than Rhian had ever seen him. He hated seeing his friend like that and wished like hell he had a clue what to do about it.

He imagined hugging Garrick. Then he swallowed hard at what the mere thought of pressing his body against Garrick did to his libido.

"Are we keeping you from something?" Alexei asked.

"What? Ah...no. Sorry." He took a deep breath. "I need to talk to Garrick about something."

Mike's smile was slow and terrifying.

Holy shit. Had something given him away?

Mike jumped in his seat, his smile disappearing as he bent over to rub his shin under the table.

"You go see Garrick," Alexei said with a big smile. "He looks like he could use a friend. We see you tomorrow."

Rhian nodded, acting as nonchalant as humanly possible. "Yeah, sure. See you guys in the morning."

Walking away, he tried to appear as though the hounds of hell and all his secrets weren't nipping at his heels. Plastering on a big smile, he approached the bar and slapped Garrick on the shoulder in an incredibly manly and totally heterosexual greeting.

The effect was ruined when Garrick met his gaze. Everything in Rhian stilled. Shifted. For the second time that day, he was pinned under the weight of Garrick's stare. He didn't move, his ass half on the bar stool, half suspended in air.

Fuck. *What the hell is this?*

Rhian blinked, wondering if he imagined Garrick's amber eyes deepening to warm chocolate.

He sat slowly, his smile fading. His mind was playing tricks on him. This was Garrick. Beautiful, hard-bodied, *straight* Garrick.

Rhian tore his gaze away and shook his head to clear it.

Garrick turned back to the TV, his undivided attention on the curling tournament, his expression grim. He chugged the rest of his beer and set the glass back on the bar with a loud crack.

Something was wrong, but Rhian had no idea what. And still he wished he could help. Fix it.

This friendship shit was confusing as hell.

All thoughts of getting drunk fled. Garrick needed to leave the bar.

Now.

The moment Rhian had touched him—a stupid, simple pat on the back, for Christ's sake—Garrick had hardened to stone. Need throbbed through his veins, arousal licking over his skin like fire. He felt hot and restless, like he was being chased by...what? By over a decade of ignoring something he wanted. By a year of wanting this man and no longer being able to pretend that wasn't true.

Savannah, what the hell have you done to me?

He stood. Abruptly. He was no fool. When a man was chased, he should run.

"Where are you going?" Rhian asked.

Garrick threw money on the bar. He couldn't get his voice to work, so he just shook his head and turned away.

"Garrick?"

The trace of hurt in Rhian's voice made Garrick feel like shit, even as it made blood pump into his cock and his feet move faster.

He had to get away. *Run.*

Rhian called his name again, but he kept going. He saw concern on Alexei and Mike's faces, but didn't stop. Didn't smile. He had no reassurances to offer anyone—least of all himself.

He had to get away. To his room.

He pressed the UP button for the elevator repeatedly until, at last, the damn doors opened. He was almost clear. Almost alone. Almost where he wouldn't have to keep his feelings from showing on his face or his erection from showing in his jeans.

Almost.

Rhian leaped onto the elevator just as the doors closed, sealing himself and Garrick into the tiny box.

He had no idea what the hell he was doing.

He should probably leave Garrick alone. It was obviously what Garrick wanted. But Rhian couldn't shake the feeling there was something going on. Something to do with Garrick's disappearances, how stressed out he'd been for the past few weeks, how tired. Garrick just wasn't himself.

Rhian didn't have the foggiest fucking idea how to help someone who seemed more than capable of taking care of himself, and who had made it pretty clear he didn't want any help. Still, he had to try.

Also, what the fuck was with those stares?

Ordering himself to settle, to focus on one thing at a time, he kept his back to the elevator doors and studied Garrick. His friend appeared a little wide-eyed. Possibly nauseated? Maybe he'd had too much to drink, which wasn't like him either.

"You okay?" Rhian asked.

The small space felt intimate. Tight.

Garrick dropped his gaze and shrugged, then shoved his hands in the pockets of his jeans. Drawn by the movement and the constant desire to look anyway, Rhian's eyes darted down to Garrick's crotch.

Hands in pockets or not, there was no way to miss the huge erection pressing against Garrick's fly. Rhian's heart rate doubled.

Shit. What did *that* mean?

Nothing. It meant nothing.

He searched Garrick's tight face and tried again. "You sure you're okay?"

Garrick stared at the lights indicating which floor they

were passing. "Fine. Just going to get some rest."

It was probably true. He'd had to be shaken awake when the bus had arrived.

Though, that still didn't explain why Garrick wouldn't look at him. Or the erection. The one Rhian couldn't stop thinking about. The one he had to look at again, as if his eyeballs had little weights on them and nothing on earth could prevent them from dropping.

Damn it. It was definitely still there.

Rhian dragged his eyes back up to find Garrick was looking at him funny.

Rhian winced. *Shit.* He'd just been caught checking out his friend's package.

He pretended with all his might he had no idea what that look was about. "What?"

The ensuing silence was deafening.

Rhian flinched when the elevator dinged. The doors opened, and Garrick charged past him and down the hall without saying a word. Rhian's nerves went from buzzing to nuclear. He held the door to the elevator open, frozen with indecision. Instinct told him to follow Garrick. To try to explain it away. Logic told him to leave the man the fuck alone.

Instinct won.

Garrick stopped at his door and fished his keycard from his pocket. When Rhian drew up beside him, Garrick's head snapped up, his eyes wide. Clearly surprised. Possibly alarmed.

Rhian was equally surprised and alarmed to see how fucking huge Garrick's cock was, pressing against the front of his jeans without Garrick's hands to disguise it.

Stop looking!

"Can I come in?"

"Why?"

Good question. What could he say? He needed to know Garrick was okay. If they were okay. He needed to explain. Or something. *Fuck.* How the hell was he going to explain checking out Garrick's dick?

Rhian looked again—*yowwee*—then up and down the hallway. "Let's talk inside."

Garrick stood unmoving, probably trying to come up with a nice way to tell Rhian to fuck off. Rhian didn't realize he was holding his breath until Garrick opened his door and walked through it. He didn't wait for Rhian, but he didn't slam the door in his face either. It was all the invitation he was going to get, so he took it.

The moment the door struck home behind Rhian, Garrick spun to face him. "Well?"

Rhian knew he shouldn't, but *had* to check again. Garrick's erection was clearly outlined by the soft denim of his beat-up jeans. Rhian pulse pounded in his ears in time with the throb in his dick. Now that he'd looked, he couldn't stop staring. It was big. Thick. And larger. Definitely larger than when he'd first noticed it in the elevator.

Rhian wanted to take it in his mouth so badly his knees went weak.

"Are you checking me out?" Garrick asked, his voice ringing with disbelief.

Rhian closed his eyes and swallowed hard. This was stupid. A mistake. A bad, bad, *bad* idea.

"Yes."

Garrick took a step back. "I don't understand. You date women."

Rhian stared pointedly at the bulge in Garrick's pants before meeting his gaze. "Yeah. So do you."

"Yeah. I do."

Rhian nodded, not sure what to say about that. Or about the fact Garrick was still standing there, staring at him, rather than throwing him out, beating him up, or denying everything.

"I'm bi," Rhian blurted. He could hardly believe the words had left his mouth.

Garrick ran his hand through his hair. Repeatedly. "Holy *shit*." He did not sound pleased.

Rhian's shoulders slumped. "Yeah. Holy shit," he echoed in a quiet voice.

He reached for the door.

Chapter Six

Garrick didn't know what he wanted. Or more precisely, what he wanted *first.*

But then, it wouldn't matter what he wanted if Rhian left.

Garrick pounced. There was no other word for it.

Grabbing Rhian's arms, he spun him around and slammed his back against the door. Garrick hadn't intended to be quite so forceful, but *fuck*, he was strung tight and winging it. Rhian's eyes bulged. Like maybe Rhian thought Garrick was going to beat the shit out of him.

Not hardly.

Garrick always tried to be a thoughtful and clever lover, but all finesse deserted him now. Giving over to his raging need, he smashed the full length of his body to Rhian's, his erection jammed against Rhian's hard belly, his thigh wedged between Rhian's and nestled up against the his junk.

Garrick watched, transfixed, as cobalt blue irises disappeared beneath dilating pupils. Pink seeped over high cheekbones. Rhian's mouth fell open and Garrick captured it, overwhelmed by the deluge of sensory input flooding into his system.

Rhian tasted sweet and sharp. Delicious. Firm, warm, and incredibly responsive lips clung to his.

Garrick moved closer, held tighter, and slipped his tongue into Rhian's eager mouth. He swallowed Rhian's moan and met the buck of his hips, desire roaring through him.

This. This was what he wanted. Needed. Only it was so much more. His normally reserved friend came alive in his arms, writhing against him, broadcasting his pleasure with little sounds in the back of his throat that Garrick instantly craved.

Garrick changed the angle of the kiss, desperate to get

closer, taste more, feel everything, find all the answers to the questions he hadn't dared ask. Coarse stubble abraded his freshly shaven chin. Strong hands clasped his hips and yanked him in tight as Rhian ground against him. It was perfect.

So much strength. So much power.

Garrick's head swam. How had he gone so long without this? How had he suppressed this need for so many years, let alone resisted this man for even one week?

He pushed and thrust and reveled in the resistance Rhian's hard-muscled body offered. No curves and soft spots here. Just angles and planes. A man.

His friend.

He slid his hands along Rhian's jaw and took control of the kiss, desperate exploration morphing into absolute possession. His pulse skipped when Rhian murmured against his lips and acquiesced completely, practically melting against the door. Against Garrick.

He feasted on Rhian's mouth, glutting himself. No lipstick, perfume, or lotion. Just the hint of sweat and piney shaving cream. A little sports rub buried in there too—which was way fucking sexier than he ever would have guessed.

Rhian jerked Garrick's shirt free of his pants, the cold air on his skin a momentary diversion. It was nothing, though, compared to Rhian's hands skimming up and over his ribs. They were calloused and so pleasingly rough as they dragged along his sensitive skin.

Tearing his mouth away, he sucked much-needed oxygen into his lungs. He grabbed Rhian's T-shirt, yanked it off and tossed it to the floor. Then he could only stop and stare.

He'd seen Rhian's chest a thousand times, but this was different. This wasn't some torturous test to see how much he could glimpse without getting caught. This was about looking his fill. At his leisure.

"You have no idea how long I've wanted to do this." He ran both hands down Rhian's chest, catching each nipple with a fingernail, learning the texture of every ridge.

Rhian's eyes fluttered closed. His voice was little more than a hoarse moan. "I do know. I can't even look at you in the locker room."

Rhian opened his eyes and looked up at Garrick with a heavy-lidded, unfocused gaze. All the hair on the back of Garrick's neck stood on end. Rhian was gorgeous all the time, but in the throes of passion, he was fucking beautiful.

Garrick needed more. More of Rhian vague-eyed and swollen-lipped. More skin. More touch. He could hardly bring himself to pull his hands away to tear his own shirt up over his head. He immediately reached for Rhian again, but stopped to let his friend's eyes trail over his chest and belly.

Rhian smoothed rough palms along Garrick's pecs and up over his shoulder. Garrick relished the large, strong hands rubbing down his back and around his ribs. He growled when Rhian's hands returned to his chest and thumbs flicked across his nipples, forcing them to bud tight and hard.

More. He slipped his fingertips behind Rhian's waistband, loving how Rhian's hard stomach jumped under his knuckles. Garrick popped the button and began to slide the zipper in a slow, delicate trip downward. His excitement careened higher with the freeing of each tooth of Rhian's fly.

Rhian's hands grasped his and halted his single-minded quest. "Wait."

Garrick would die of frustration if Rhian made him stop now. He tore his gaze from their joined hands and searched Rhian's face. "What is it?"

"We can't," Rhian gasped, his breathing hectic, his regret palpable. "Fuck, I want to, but I can't. I like Savannah. You're my friend. I don't want to fuck up...God, this *sucks.*"

Garrick dropped his chin to his chest and fought to clear his head. He needed to explain, quickly and succinctly, so they could get back to the more interesting task of ripping each other's clothes off.

He met Rhian's deep blue gaze. "It's okay. I cannot believe I'm about to admit this, but it was her idea."

"Pardon me?" Rhian asked, completely expressionless.

"This. You. Me. I mean, she didn't know it would be you or that it would be tonight or—*shit*." He was making a real hash of this explanation. "Savannah knows I'm attracted to men. Or I was. Have been in the past." Garrick sighed. This sounded only marginally less insane in his head. "Look, here's what it is. I'm bi, too. Savannah knows. She doesn't want me to be lonely while we're apart and said I could sleep with another person as long as that other person is a man and I tell her about it."

Rhian's dubious look proved Garrick hadn't successfully avoided his sanity being called into question. "Say what?"

Laughing, Garrick pressed his forehead to Rhian's, daring to steal a quick kiss, pleased when Rhian's lips briefly clung to his. "That's what I said too. But then I started thinking, you know, about you, and how I haven't been thinking about it because we play hockey, and I assumed you were straight, and then I was thinking about it even though I shouldn't, and then I tried to get drunk and you tried to console me, which didn't help at all, so I ran, you followed, and here the fuck we are."

Garrick grimaced. His goal of being concise had definitely been lost somewhere. He thought he'd at least gotten his point across. And Rhian seemed to be taking it well. He wasn't running. Or laughing hysterically.

"Shit. Savannah is quite a woman, isn't she?"

Garrick smiled at the quiet awe in Rhian's voice. "Yes, she is. This is only one of the many reasons why I am in love with her."

Rhian took a moment to digest that, and while Garrick would have been bitterly disappointed and monumentally frustrated to walk away at this point, Rhian deserved the truth.

"Are you okay with this?" Garrick asked.

Rhian looked up and Garrick fell into his dark blue gaze. He'd never wanted a man more in his life.

"As long as no one is cheating." There was a hint of a question in Rhian's voice.

Garrick's smile was slow. "No one is cheating."

"Then yes, I'm—"

Garrick captured Rhian's mouth and thrust his tongue past Rhian's still-parted lips. After a grunt of surprise, Rhian gave himself over, his hands curling around Garrick's neck and holding on.

Garrick blindly finished unzipping Rhian's pants and shoved them down over lean hips, satisfied when they thumped to the floor.

No underwear. Shit, that was hot.

But not half as hot as Rhian's thick cock. Garrick ended their kiss so he could look. At last. The mushroom-shaped crown was flushed dark crimson, the veins along the shaft standing out in stark relief against the pale, silky skin beneath. Garrick's mouth watered and his ass clenched. He didn't know where to begin.

While Garrick stood there in a daze, unable to tear his eyes away, Rhian kicked his shoes and pants aside and unfastened Garrick's jeans. He wasn't prepared when Rhian stole his move from earlier and spun, checking Garrick back into the door. He slammed against the hard wood, still warm from Rhian's broad shoulders.

There weren't a lot of people who could manhandle Garrick. That a man every bit as strong and physical as he— possibly more—was about to become his lover was unbelievably fucking hot.

Then Rhian fell to his knees, taking Garrick's jeans, boxer briefs, and every single goddamn thought in his head along with him.

His painfully hard cock sprang free, yanking a grunt from his chest. The exquisitely sensitive head brushed Rhian's soft, dark blond curls and cheek before coming to rest not a hair's breadth from Rhian's full, red lips.

"Perfect," Rhian whispered. He brushed a finger along the slit, gathering the pre-come waiting there, then dipped his finger into his mouth.

Garrick made another noise, this one embarrassingly like a gurgle. He watched, stupefied, as Rhian leaned forward and ran his tongue over the same spot his finger had just touched. Hot breath washed over Garrick's cock.

Almost insensible with anticipation, Garrick's entire cognitive function boiled down to *ohmysweetjesuspleasepleasepleasepleasejustdoitgodPLEASE.*

He wobbled, almost falling to the floor when his knees turned to jelly. Wrapping one hand around the doorjamb, he watched wide-eyed as Rhian Savage, the fastest, toughest defensemen in the EHL, closed his eyes in apparent bliss and licked away more pre-come. Electric shocks fired through Garrick's body, searing him from the inside out. He was pitifully close to coming. So close to painting that beautiful face with his thick white seed, he had to clutch the doorframe until his fingers ached, amazed it didn't crack under the pressure.

Rhian continued his torment. Gentle licks brushed Garrick's shaft, jolting through him like fire. Needy little noises caught in the back of Rhian's throat with each lick, as if it were Rhian's dick being worshipped. Garrick twitched in reaction to each sound. He didn't know how much longer he could take it, could stand still and not touch.

Rhian slid the crown into his mouth, swirled his tongue around it once, then sank down the shaft, his mouth forced open wide.

Garrick's control slipped. He fisted a hand in Rhian's curls, knowing he held on just a little too tightly. He couldn't help it. He had almost no command left over his own body, having relinquished it entirely into Rhian's care.

Rhian's mouth stretched, his lips thinning as he continued to take more of Garrick into his mouth. Down his throat. The heat, the pressure, the *need*, was almost unbearable.

Sweet Jesus. Garrick was not a small man, in any respect. No one had ever taken this much. Taken it all. The air burned in his lungs when his straining, swollen head bumped the back of Rhian's throat, then slid farther, until Rhian's lips were wrapped around the base of his shaft. Wet warmth enveloped Garrick from tip to stem, exciting him beyond measure. His chest locked up, his entire body frozen. He was terrified to move. To breathe. Perhaps it was empathy, as there was no way Rhian could breathe with Garrick's cock lodged so deep.

The trust was humbling. And a huge fucking turn-on.

Garrick was dimly aware he'd gone up on the balls of his feet, his body plastered to the door, petrified he'd lose control and start thrusting the way every instinct in his body screamed at him to do.

Then Rhian swallowed.

"God, Rhian! *Fuck!*" Garrick howled. His hips shot forward before banging back against the door. He shuddered. Again and again.

Rhian eased off, his cheeks hollowing out, sucking Garrick's brains right out through his cock. His balls drew up tight, ready to concede, the battle lost to Rhian's spectacular mouth. He wanted to fuck, to plunge in and out until he poured himself down that ridiculously talented throat.

Who is this man? This generous, passionate lover who Garrick had thought he'd known so well. He would never see Rhian the same way again. Not because his feelings had lessened—quite the opposite—but because it was if the mask had been torn off. In this moment, Rhian was new to him. Gorgeous. Changed.

Garrick tried to capture all he could, to file away every detail. His memory was forever seared with the image of those full lips wrapped around his cock.

Rhian opened his eyes, looked right up at Garrick, and smiled.

"Fuck. *Fuck.*" His reverent whisper wasn't going to win any awards for poetry, but it was all he had.

Rhian's laughter was no more than a vibration against Garrick's skin, spiraling around his shaft and punching through his gut.

Rhian plunged deep again and Garrick could do little more than moan. And feel. Rhian's hand wrapped around the base of his cock, twisting as he sucked his way up Garrick's length before sinking down once more. On the deepest plunges, he'd pull his hand away and pause. Then swallow. On the furthest retreats, his hot tongue laved the underside of Garrick's shaft, rubbing along the throbbing vein, until just the tip tickled the divot at the top.

Garrick couldn't stop the pitch and roll of his hips any more than he could have stopped the tide from coming in. He fucked Rhian's mouth and Rhian took it, adjusting to meet each push, barely missing a beat to accommodate the hectic thrusts.

The tingles crawling up Garrick's spine began to coalesce, knotting deep within him. He tried to give a warning, hardly achieving more than grunts. "Shit. I'm going to come. Rhian, I'm g-g-gonna…"

Rhian didn't pull off. He sank all the way down, his fingers digging into Garrick's thighs the only restraint he offered. He swallowed hard, soft muscles clenching, undulating, dragging Garrick over the edge.

"*Rhian!*"

Climax heaved up and out of him and spilled down Rhian's throat. Garrick's head slammed back against the door, but he was already seeing stars behind his eyelids. Rhian's strong hands held his hips in place. Held him up. His wicked mouth demanded everything Garrick had. Relentless.

Garrick gave it gladly.

Chapter Seven

Rhian sat back on his heels and watched Garrick try to catch his breath. He'd never really believed the old adage about how it made a difference when you cared.

Now he knew better.

Poking out his tongue, he swept up a little bit of Garrick's come from his lower lip but stopped mid-lick when Garrick whimpered, staring at Rhian's mouth with wide eyes. Rhian smiled. He was mighty pleased with the results of his hard work. It was glaringly apparent Garrick needed some time to regain all his faculties.

Rhian chuckled as he rose to his feet.

Leaving Garrick pinned to the door like it was coated with fly paper, he wandered deeper into the room. Not that there was far to go. Two strides and he was beside the bed *and* the desk.

He was contemplating the laptop, almost lost among the mountain of papers and folders on the desk, when strong hands clamped around his right arm and left thigh.

What the hell is—holy shit! Rhian was airborne.

He landed on his back on the bed in an undignified sprawl, his breath leaving him in a loud whoosh.

He barely bounced before Garrick was above him, caging him with his hands and knees. He leaned his face in close and captured Rhian's undivided attention with his warm brown gaze. "Nice move earlier, pinning me to the door."

Rhian's throat clicked, he gulped so hard.

"At the very least, there has to be…" Garrick paused, dragging in a deep breath as if scenting the air between them. "…*retaliation*." The word rolled off Garrick's tongue, his voice little more than a deep purr.

Shivers coursed over Rhian's entire body. They had

nothing to do with fear of what Garrick promised and everything to do with arousal. Needs long suppressed.

Rhian's cock twitched, painting a shiny line across Garrick's hard belly. The drag of the achingly sensitive head against Garrick's smooth skin turned shivers into shudders. Garrick's hot stare, the promise in his voice, his size, his strength, all fired Rhian's imagination. His body flushed with need, his face burning, his tongue tied with the almost uncontrollable desire to blurt out everything he wanted.

He was doing a damn poor job of hiding his response. He didn't care. The smile whispering across Garrick's handsome face triggered curls of warm arousal to tighten in his belly. His balls. Anticipation ratcheted up to near painful, perfect levels. He didn't know what Garrick wanted to do. Would do. But Rhian wanted it. More than his next breath, he wanted it.

Garrick dropped slowly and pressed Rhian into the bed. His heart pounded as Garrick's palms slid down his arms and over his hands, still splayed from his landing. Long fingers curled around his, forcing him to grasp the comforter.

Their lips barely brushed when Garrick spoke.

"Don't let go."

Rhian licked his suddenly dry lips. "Why not?" His voice was a whisper. It hurt to talk.

Strong hands clenched tighter. "Because I said so."

Holy fuck.

Rhian's hips rocked upward and dragged his cock along the hard planes of Garrick's stomach. He nodded quickly when Garrick lifted one brow. He didn't so much as twitch a muscle when Garrick let go of his arms and wrapped both hands around his face.

Rhian forgot to breathe, wide-eyed and frozen in place as Garrick slowly came closer.

His tongue teased across Rhian's swollen, tender lips, soothing them before slipping into his mouth. His eyes slid shut, his tongue dancing slowly with Garrick's. Strong hands held his jaw gently. Their noses brushed. The unexpected and incredible tenderness heightened Rhian's hyper-awareness of his immobility. His arms trembled with the desire to thrust his fingers through Garrick's hair and hold on.

He didn't. Wouldn't.

Garrick released his mouth with a last pull to his lower lip.

Rhian moaned at the loss as Garrick rose and cold air swept over him. He wanted desperately to grab Garrick and drag him back. He clutched the comforter harder.

Garrick slid down Rhian's body. Lips brushed behind his ear. Sharp teeth scraped down his neck to sink into the spot where it met his shoulder. Rhian writhed with each touch, his back arching when Garrick soothed the bite mark with a touch of his tongue.

He moved lower, licking a slow path to one nipple. Then the next. More back-arching, blood humming ecstasy roared through Rhian. He jolted each time Garrick drew one of the sensitive nubs between his lips and sucked hard, a thumb and finger pinching the other in time with the pull of Garrick's hot mouth.

Rhian thrashed against the bed. His cock tapped between their bellies, each contact another shock through his body. His shifting legs ran along Garrick's long, hard inner thighs. Coarse hair rubbed and tickled, adding another layer of sensation.

Rhian, though barely rational, still recognized it would be a little embarrassing to come from nothing more than Garrick playing with his nipples.

"Garrick, please." He didn't recognize his own voice.

Garrick's mouth skimmed along the underside of his pecs. Rhian felt warm lips curve into a smile. Garrick's eyes creased at the corners when he looked up. Apparently, he liked it when Rhian begged.

Rhian liked it, too.

His reward was even better. Garrick's long fingers spread wide across his ribs, thumbs tracing the bumps of his abs on their way south. He arched into the touch, hoping to hell that those hands were headed to his cock. They trailed down his sensitive belly and separated, bypassing his shaft to wrap around his hips instead.

Rhian groaned. The sound was pathetic and needy. And honest.

Garrick shifted forward and pressed Rhian's ass against the mattress, pinning him to the bed.

Rhian was keenly aware of the picture he made as Garrick stared down at him. His cock pearled with pre-come while his chest heaved to gather enough air to stay sane. And still his trembling arms stayed locked in place.

Garrick's heavy-lidded gaze lifted, spearing straight into him. His lips were red and swollen, his chin and cheeks pink from Rhian's heavy stubble. Rhian stared back.

As the seconds ticked past, the surging rush to completion still grappled in his guts, in his balls, but his hectic breathing evened out. His frantic pulse leveled to a steady throb, the blood in his veins thickening until the ponderous beat of his heart drummed in his head, his chest, and his cock, in a single beat.

He could not move. He could not act. Take. Give. Touch.

He could only feel. And trust.

Even in the midst of this mind-boggling passion, he knew these were not things he did well. He'd spent the better part of his life trying not to feel, always failing miserably. He'd learned he wasn't capable of shutting off his emotions, so instead he'd shut himself off from other people. Trusted no one. He'd learned this lesson countless times. Had it beaten into him— literally and figuratively—throughout his childhood.

But here, now, with his friend, it wasn't really a question. There was no hurdle to clear. Not anymore. Whatever obstacles Rhian had thrown up had long since been conquered.

Size and strength were not what held him pinned to the bed. Nor did the threat of retaliation—whether physical or sexual, pleasurable or painful—keep him immobile.

It was trust. Friendship. The absolute certainty that Garrick would not willingly hurt or knowingly betray him.

For the very first time in Rhian's life, he found refuge in another person.

It was absolutely fucking terrifying.

Some hint of his fear, his confusion, must have shown on his face. Or maybe Garrick felt his body fall out of the collected rhythm Rhian had treasured moments ago. Garrick came closer, slowly, and rubbed his face against Rhian's cheek. His lips brushed Rhian's ear.

"Do you want me to let go?" he asked quietly.

Rhian held still, acutely aware of the brush of Garrick's thick eyelashes against the delicate skin of his eyelid. The press of Garrick's thumbs on his hipbones. The heavy musk of Garrick's arousal on his own skin.

But it was Garrick's deep voice that settled him.

"No. Don't let go."

Garrick waited, unmoving, and Rhian feared Garrick might do it anyway. Or ask if Rhian was okay. He honestly didn't have an answer for that, so he turned his head and dragged his lips against Garrick's in clear invitation. He didn't kiss him. Just...*offered*.

Garrick accepted.

In spite of the sure knowledge that he was navigating an emotional minefield for which he had never been given a map, Rhian sank into the kiss, giving himself over. Entrusting himself to Garrick.

Garrick's tongue slid slowly over his, his lips rubbing back and forth as if gentling him.

They kissed as if they had all night. As if this was all they'd come here for. And maybe it was. But as much as Rhian was enjoying it, the hum of urgency built in his chest, the steady throb of arousal returning in force as Garrick held him to the bed and kissed him tenderly.

He groaned against Garrick's lips. "*Please.*"

Garrick sat back and dragged his gaze down over Rhian's body, stopping when he got to his cock. Garrick's tongue swept out to moisten his lips and Rhian whimpered, every cell in his body screaming for Garrick to touch him.

Garrick dropped his head slowly and the crown of Rhian's cock disappeared into Garrick's mouth, bathed in a hot breath a moment before those gorgeous lips closed around the sensitive ridge. A powerful suck bowed his spine between the anchors of his hips and hands, still firmly on the bed. The broad flat of Garrick's tongue whisked across the head, rubbing over a bazillion electrified nerve endings.

Rhian's body lit up, every muscle straining. The instinct to fuck Garrick's mouth battled against his immobilization and lost. His kept his hips where Garrick had put them and threw his head back to shout his pleasure.

"Garrick!" His voice broke over the name.

Garrick released Rhian's cock with a lewd pop and took up a torturous series of licks down the shaft. He spread his knees, pushing Rhian's thighs apart.

He opened to Garrick without question or hesitation. Garrick's lips traveled lower, mouthing Rhian's firm sac. Rhian groaned, his eyes rolling back in his head. Garrick's mouth was hot, his teeth the barest scrape. He wrapped his lips around one ball but it was drawn so tightly against Rhian's body that Garrick couldn't pull it into his mouth.

With a final lick, he nibbled his way back up to the crown, ending with a long, slow rasp of tongue.

Everything in Rhian clenched tight, ready to explode. Garrick pulled him into his mouth and sucked in earnest. He released his hold on Rhian's hips and wrapped a hand around the base of his cock, adding more pressure and movement, and preventing Rhian from forcing himself too deeply into his mouth.

He needn't have worried. Rhian was locked up tight, his body rigid, muscles clenched, his orgasm coming on like a freight train. Garrick slipped a finger into his mouth, then pulled it free and bumped it over the tight pucker of Rhian's anus, making slow circles until just the tip eased in.

Rhian burst into a million little pieces.

It was a long time before the intense swells of his orgasm were replaced with a wash of euphoria that left Rhian limp, his body melting into the bed. He never wanted to move from this spot. He never wanted to forget what this felt like.

Even in his post-coital haze, he knew that he should get up and leave. He couldn't spend the night, and he didn't imagine Garrick would want him to.

He was almost ready to actually use a muscle and lift his head from the mattress when Garrick dragged him to the top of the bed and yanked the covers out from underneath them. The bed shifted, the lights snapped off, and Rhian didn't know what the hell to think.

Maybe Garrick was ready for another round?

A strong arm wrapped around his ribs and hauled him across the bed. He ended up with his ass tucked against the tops of Garrick's thighs and Garrick's chest warming his back. Rhian held perfectly still while he tried to figure out what the fuck was going on. Garrick's hand dropped to his belly and soothed his skin in broad strokes, his fingers stopping everyone once in a while to trace patterns in the little hairs of his treasure trail.

Holy shit, were they *snuggling*?

With a couple pokes, Garrick rearranged them so Rhian was using Garrick's arm as a pillow, his nose pressed to Garrick's biceps, the smell of warm skin and *Garrick* familiar and strange.

But then, this whole damn thing was strange. Rhian had never snuggled, spooned, cuddled, *whatever* in his life. Sure, he'd slept in the same bed, curled up with the other kids in some of the houses. But that was about safety in numbers.

This was about...

What the hell is *this about?*

His mind raced to come up with a reason to get out of bed. A way to ask Garrick to let him go. But the fingers dancing against his skin kept pulling his thoughts off course. The steady rhythm of Garrick's heart against his back lulled him.

Garrick would probably fall asleep quickly. Rhian decided he would sneak out after that.

It was his last thought before he slipped into a deep, peaceful sleep.

Chapter Eight

Garrick woke the next morning, sorry to leave behind the most blissful uninterrupted night's sleep he'd had in weeks.

Where the hell was he?

Then he remembered. On a road trip. The hotel. The bar.

Rhian.

With a start, he opened his eyes to find his friend, *his lover*, curled into his chest. Rhian's breathing was deep and even. He looked peaceful. Calm. Hardly like the ball of nerves Garrick had pulled into his arms last night.

It had taken a solid ten minutes of petting to get Rhian to relax. After an orgasm like that, the man should have succumbed to sleep in a heartbeat. He'd certainly appeared more than ready to snooze when he'd been sprawled out across the mattress after Garrick had finished with him.

But by the time Garrick had tucked them in together, Rhian had gone rigid with tension. Garrick could have let the guy off the hook and allowed him to leave. He would have if Rhian had asked, of course. Even just once.

But he hadn't asked. And Garrick hadn't offered. Seeing him like this, he was glad he hadn't.

Rhian's curls stood up in all directions, his thick lashes casting dark shadows on his cheeks in the half light. No lack of illumination could disguise his high cheekbones or the soft pink cushion of his lower lip. The muscles in his neck and cheeks were lax, making Garrick realize how tightly Rhian held himself when he was awake.

Asleep, he didn't look like he had a care in the world. He looked...*young.*

Twenty-four years old. Garrick winced. Except, never in the time they'd been friends had Rhian's age been an issue. He was what Garrick's mom would call an *old soul.*

He traced a finger over the barely discernible lines radiating from the corners of Rhian's eyes. They popped when he smiled, but Garrick had seen them more often when Rhian's face was creased with worry or stress. And they were deep enough to make Garrick wonder how much time he'd spent doing either in his relatively short years.

Rhian never complained. Never blamed anyone but himself for anything. He was kind, smart. A fucking brilliant hockey player. Garrick knew these things. And little else.

He sure as shit hadn't guessed Rhian was bi. A fact Garrick couldn't be happier about.

With that thought foremost in his mind, he tried to decide the best way to wake his lover. Rhian was obviously a deep sleeper, since the little touches Garrick had run across his skin hadn't roused him at all.

He considered some much more interesting touches and discovered Rhian *had* been roused after all. He just hadn't yet woken up.

Excellent.

Garrick slid his hand beneath the sheets slowly, uncurling his fingers to grasp—

Three loud knocks at his door startled Garrick and he snatched his hand back as if he'd been caught being naughty. And he supposed he had. He grinned.

Three more knocks.

Who the fuck is it?

Stumbling to his feet, he yanked on his pants and struggled to get his brain in gear. He couldn't just open his door. Certainly no one was going to miss the six foot two, two hundred and some-odd pound defenseman tangled in his sheets. And while he found he cared far less than he should have about that possibility, he had to protect Rhian. At all costs.

He gathered up Rhian's clothes, chucked them into the closet and shut the door. Hoping to muffle some of the sounds inside his room, he cranked on the shower and left the door to the hallway open.

Three more knocks.

"I'm coming!"

He suddenly remembered the last time he'd shouted those very words in this very hallway and smiled grimly. He had to get rid of whoever the fuck was at his door. He had better things to do this morning. *Way* better things.

Speaking of which, he rushed back to the bed to wake Rhian and found him sitting up, the sheets pooled in his lap. He looked sleepy. Confused. And once again, *young.*

"Goddamn, I'm too old for you," Garrick muttered quietly, afraid the noise from the shower wouldn't sufficiently mask their voices if they spoke normally.

The confusion cleared from Rhian's face, replaced by a lopsided grin. "Safe to say you proved otherwise last night." His voice was little more than a rasp. It sounded...damaged. Garrick's cock flooded with blood, even as he cringed with remorse.

"Are you okay?"

Rhian coughed to clear his throat. "I'm fine." It still sounded like he had full-blown laryngitis.

Whoever was out in the hall pounded on his door again.

Garrick leaned in and pressed a hard kiss to Rhian's mouth. "Hurry," he said in a furious whisper. "Go get in the shower."

Rhian leaped from the bed and dashed into the bathroom. Garrick admired the flex of that glorious ass the whole way across the room. *Damn.*

Smoothing a hand over the front of his pants, he conjured images of his elderly elementary school art teacher, Mrs. Plum. Worked every time.

He pulled the bathroom door shut and cracked the door to the hallway.

In the rush to get all evidence of Rhian hidden, Garrick hadn't bothered to guess who the hell might be banging on his door so early in the morning. But even if he'd had days to think about it, he wouldn't have come up with the guy Rhian had been arguing with in the lobby last night.

"Can I help you?" he asked, pretending not to recognize him.

"Hey, yeah. Sorry it's so early. But have you seen Rhian?"

Garrick's heart lodged somewhere around his windpipe. Did Rhian tell this guy about them?

As quickly as the worry arrived, it fled. When Rhian had been in the lobby last night, neither one of them had any idea they'd end up here this morning. And Rhian wasn't stupid. They both knew the reality was that any team would hesitate to draft a player if a media shit-storm might come along with him.

The stranger's expression changed from innocent inquiry to narrow-eyed speculation.

"No," Garrick blurted, kicking himself for the long pause while he screwed his head on straight. "I haven't seen him since last night. In the bar. About nine o'clock." Garrick snapped his mouth shut and swore to himself he'd someday learn to lie well.

"His agent is looking for him."

"And who are you?" *And how the fuck did you get my room number? And why?*

"Steve. His brother."

Garrick must have looked as shocked as he felt.

"Well, sort of. Whatever." Steve scowled. "Listen, if you see him, tell him to call Sergio. His agent."

Garrick knew who the fuck Sergio was.

"Anyway, he's here," Steve said. "Says he can't find Rhian. He's not in his room and he's not answering his cell."

No sooner had the words sprung from Steve's lips that a rhythmic buzz emanated from the closet. Garrick prayed Steve couldn't hear it.

"If I see him, I'll let him know." He *refused* to ask Steve why he'd come here searching for Rhian. He had every intention of asking Rhian about it, though. Could Steve be his boyfriend?

No, Rhian wouldn't cheat. An ex-boyfriend? Was the brother thing their cover? If so, it was a stupid one. This guy didn't look a thing like the beautiful man standing in Garrick's shower. Steve had dark hair and beady eyes. He reminded Garrick of a rat.

The idea that he and Rhian might have been intimate turned Garrick's stomach inside out, but he kept his face blank.

Steve shrugged, sending Garrick one last speculative glance before walking away. Garrick shut the door and took a deep steadying breath.

Shit. That was close.

Rhian stood behind the bathroom door, heart pounding, palms sweating, and listened to Garrick try to get Steve to go the fuck away. He couldn't decide what was worse, the threat of being caught, or that he was going to have to give Garrick more of an explanation about Steve than he'd intended to last night.

That explanation came with a can of worms Rhian had hoped he'd never have to open again. In the past five years, he'd gotten comfortable being the person he was now, and not dragging around all the shit that had come before. He wouldn't be able to stand it if Garrick looked at him with pity or horror.

This much was certain—he would never forgive Steve for bringing his past, bringing himself, to Garrick's doorstep.

Garrick closed the door to the hallway and Rhian stepped out of the bathroom, determined to get it over with and get the hell out. Garrick put a finger over his lips, grabbed his pants from the closet, and pushed them both back into the bathroom, shutting them inside.

Rhian opened his mouth to offer an explanation, but his words got stuck in his throat when Garrick oh-so-casually whipped off his pants, adjusted the water temperature and shoved Rhian into the shower.

Hot water stung his skin, but Garrick was there, drawing him close, their bodies pressed together from chest to knee, and Rhian didn't give a shit if the water scalded him raw. It was damn near impossible to remember what he was going to say. He gave into the wild hope that physical needs would trump the discussion all together.

"Be careful," Garrick murmured into his ear, sending a shiver down his neck. "I don't know how much our voices echo in here. It should be safe to talk quietly."

So much for that hope. Not that Rhian blamed Garrick for wanting some answers. Rhian *was* surprised his dick didn't care more. He was as hard as stone, his cock jammed against Garrick's hip. Garrick was in a similar state. Too bad neither of them would stay that way once Garrick heard all of Rhian's stupid shit.

Garrick turned them so the spray hit Rhian's back and ran over his shoulders to cascade between their bodies. It was distracting as hell until he caught Garrick's unwavering gaze.

"I'm sorry." His ravaged voice was little more than a rasp. Keeping quiet was going to be easy for him, at least.

Garrick arched one eyebrow.

"He's not my brother," Rhian said. It was as good a place as any to begin. "I lived with him for a while, and for some reason, he's decided to put more significance on that than anyone else would."

Garrick's brows drew together. "He was your boyfriend?"

"What?" Rhian tried to step back.

Garrick didn't let go. "You said you lived together—"

"Oh, no. *No.*" Rhian would have laughed if the idea weren't so creepy. Not to mention that Rhian had never had a boyfriend. Or a girlfriend, for that matter. "No. Steve and I lived in a foster home together. In Chicago. When I was in high school, right up until I got drafted into the juniors."

He watched Garrick's face closely for his reaction.

"Foster care?"

"Since I was five."

Garrick cocked his head to one side. Rhian could practically see the questions hovering on the tip of Garrick's tongue.

He tried to ease back. He didn't get an inch.

He *had* succeeded in killing both their erections though.

"I'm sorry," Garrick said simply, his gaze direct, without pity or suspicion.

Relief loosened some of the knots in Rhian's back and neck.

"There's nothing to be sorry about. I think I came out all right." This had been his stock answer since he'd been far too young to have any idea *how* he'd turn out. He didn't follow it with his usual bullshit about how it hadn't been a big deal. Just this once, he didn't want to lie.

He flinched when Garrick's hand cupped his jaw. Garrick's thumb traced over his wet cheekbone. It was strangely intimate, this act of comfort. Before this morning, the only people Rhian had ever discussed his upbringing with had been sitting behind a desk, billing the Illinois state mental health insurance boatloads of money.

"You came out better than all right," Garrick murmured.

Rhian blinked steam and water from his eyes. That might have been the nicest thing anyone had every said to him. He clamped his mouth shut, afraid of what might come out.

Garrick shifted and their flagging erections slid over warm, wet skin. Garrick's big hand cupped Rhian's ass and shifted him closer. Higher.

Rhian broke his silence with an inarticulate gurgle.

Garrick chuckled. Rhian didn't mind. It felt too fucking good. He had the insane urge to grab Garrick and hug him. Just wrap his arms around him and bury his face against that broad shoulder and squeeze the shit out of him.

He didn't, of course. He couldn't even understand where the idea came from.

Garrick rolled his hips again, and Rhian's focus shifted to more pressing concerns. Specifically, to the concerns pressing between their bodies.

This, at least, he understood.

Chapter Nine

Garrick sat on the bench in front of his temporary locker in Charlottetown and silently fumed.

Rhian was avoiding him.

Garrick cast yet another glance over his shoulder.

Rhian was so *thoroughly* avoiding him, he'd taken a locker on the dead opposite side of the room, sandwiched between Tim and Dave.

Garrick gritted his teeth and pulled his eyes back where they belonged. He caught Alexei watching him with a little smile on his face and pointedly ignored him.

What the fuck was that about?

It had to be nothing, since no one had seen Rhian tear out of his hotel room that morning two days ago, and certainly there hadn't been anything to see since. Garrick had found it impossible to get anywhere close to Rhian except on the ice or the bench at games. Not exactly the time or place for a heated discussion between lovers.

Son of a bitch.

Garrick shoved his equipment into his bag. He'd love to wring the stupid kid's neck. He'd never thought of Rhian as a kid before, but he was one immature dumb fuck to let one night of admittedly mind-blowing sex freak him out to the point that he'd screw their friendship. Hell, if the guy didn't want to do something like that again, all he had to do was say so. It wasn't like Garrick was going to force it.

Though he could be very, *very* persuasive.

Goddamn it, he wasn't done. Garrick wasn't sure what else he wanted, but as he and Rhian had furiously jerked each other off in the shower that morning, he hadn't been thinking goodbye. He'd been thinking *heeelllo!*

Then to sit and listen to Rhian lie to Sergio about where

he'd been and arrange to meet him in the lobby, it had all been kind of illicit and hot. Especially when Rhian had made up some story about catching a cold to explain his voice.

As Rhian had said after hanging up, it wasn't like he could tell anyone he'd somehow damaged his voice deep-throating the Ice Cats' power forward's ginormous cock.

Garrick had laughed, enjoying the blush on Rhian's cheeks and trying not to wallow in the *ginormous* thing. Though, really, he was human. And a guy. So *come on.*

He'd let Rhian out of his room after checking the hallway, never guessing it would be the last time he'd see Rhian alone for days.

It was infuriating. And made Garrick sick with worry. He liked Rhian and wanted to remain his friend. Now he faced the prospect of calling Savannah and confessing all, for what might turn out to have been a terrible idea.

She'd had games on the west coast the last two nights, but tonight she was in Boston, and he would be back in his hotel room within the half hour.

Plenty of time for his nerves to churn. He was terrified that she hadn't meant what she'd said, that she'd changed her mind and not told him yet, that what had sounded like fun in theory was a disaster for her in reality.

It sure as hell hadn't been a disaster for Garrick until Rhian had tucked tail and run.

Scrubbing his hands through his hair, he turned his head and saw Alexei speaking quietly with Mike. When they both glanced at him, he stared them down until they turned away.

What the fuck was with those two gossiping like a couple of old ladies?

Whatever. Garrick had much bigger fish to fry tonight.

He charged out of the locker room to the bus and threw himself into a seat to wait for the rest of the team to load up. Rhian appeared at the front of the aisle and sat by himself a few rows up. Garrick ground his teeth. *Let it go.* They'd be home in Moncton tomorrow night. He'd deal with Rhian then. Maybe he'd just show up at his house and…

Shit. He had no idea where Rhian lived. Garrick searched his memory long and hard. The guy must have at least mentioned the neighborhood. The street. Something.

When he came up blank, he scowled out the window. What the fuck was it with Rhian and all the secrecy?

Then he remembered what Rhian had told him about his childhood, and Garrick deflated in his seat. Something in Rhian's eyes had forced Garrick to hold his tongue and not ask the questions that had been burning in his throat. He'd assumed he'd have time later to learn more about that. About Rhian. He'd planned to do it subtly.

He could practically hear Savannah laughing at him for that.

So subtlety wasn't his strong suit. But any idiot would have seen that to ask Rhian anything would have been to poke wounds he wasn't ready to let Garrick see, let alone dig at.

Maybe that was why Rhian had run?

The idea popped into his head out of nowhere, dampening the ire that had been steadily growing for two days. Maybe it wasn't the sex that freaked Rhian out. Maybe it was the intimacy.

Garrick had to admit, when Savannah had proposed he take a lover, he had not anticipated anything like what had happened between him and Rhian. He'd imagined finding someone strictly for wall-banging, teeth-rattling sex. And he sure as shit *had* found that. But he'd also imagined a stranger, or at least not a friend. And certainly not someone with whom he had a connection like the one he had with Rhian.

Something about the guy tugged at Garrick. He didn't get it, but he couldn't deny it had given their encounter an intensity that went beyond just sex.

This, more than any particular act, had him worried sick about calling Savannah.

In what felt like a matter of seconds, they were back at the hotel. Garrick marched through the lobby and up to his room without looking for Rhian once. His determination delivered him to his hotel room, alone with his cell phone and nothing to do but call Savannah, in far too little time.

Crap.

Reminding himself that he'd had her explicit permission, he dialed her number. She picked up instantly.

"Hello, stranger."

The sound of her voice went a long way toward settling his nerves. Slowly, he stripped off his clothes and lay down on the bed while they chatted about their respective road trips and general team bullshit.

It was normal. Nice.

He eyed the pile of paperwork on his desk. He had more than one confession to make. "I'm fucking up, Sav."

"How so?"

He liked that she didn't immediately leap to his defense with lots of "no, no, I'm sure you're not," but asked the question first.

"I'm struggling," he admitted. "Putting off tough decisions. Letting my feelings for people get in the way of what's best for the team. Knowing it and doing it anyway, which is somehow worse than just doing it."

She chuckled.

He was about to inform her nothing was funny about any of this, stung that she was amused, when she interrupted his growing tantrum.

"You're still you."

That completely derailed him. "Huh?"

"You're still you, Garrick." She said it as if explaining something, without censure. "You're friends with these men. You care about them. Of course you're hesitating to do things that might have a negative impact on their lives. You know their hopes, their dreams, and you *care* about those things."

Garrick lay flat on this back and stared at the cracked ceiling of his hotel room. This was not making him feel better.

His silence must have communicated as much. Her sigh reached him down the phone line. "Honey, give yourself a break. I'm not saying that in two or three years, when you know fewer of your players personally, it will be any easier. But you've carved yourself about as tough a path as anyone could, starting your first venture into management and ownership with a team staffed with your friends."

He hadn't really considered that when he'd been scrambling to find a way to buy—and save—the team. For a second he thought it might have made a difference, then he got over himself.

"You have a point." It did make him feel less stupid about being so conflicted, even if it didn't make him any *less* conflicted.

"I know you'll do the right thing, Garrick."

Whatever the fuck the right thing is. "Thank you."

That she didn't offer her opinion, while handing him her absolute faith, meant the world. It was time to live up to that faith.

"I have other news," he began carefully.

"Oh?"

He couldn't figure out what to say. Apparently, that was all the hint she needed.

She inhaled sharply. "Oh!"

For the life of him he couldn't tell if that was shock, excitement, or horror in her voice. He held his breath until she started to laugh.

"Well, for god's sake, are you going to tell me about it? We had a deal, you know."

Garrick sighed and closed his eyes. Relief flooded him. "Are you sure?"

"Am I—? Garrick, I'm *fine*."

Garrick grinned at the ceiling. "I love you."

"I love you too," she said quickly. She sounded sincere, and like she sincerely didn't want to talk about it at the moment. "Now spill."

He chuckled. "Uhhh…"

"Garrick!"

"No, I'm not stalling. I swear. I don't know where to start."

She practically purred. "That sounds promising. Start at the beginning. Where did you meet him?"

"Well, actually," he said, realizing the single most shocking thing he had to tell her was probably the identity of his lover. He was still a little shocked by it himself. "It's Rhian."

"Rhian?"

"Yeah."

"Rhian who? Not… *Oh my god*. Please don't tell me you mean *Rhian Savage*." She sounded like she was begging him to do just that.

He chuckled. "The one."

It was her turn to fall silent. Garrick wondered what she was thinking.

Then she let out a long, almost painful sounding moan. "I think I'm jealous."

Garrick bolted upright. "What?"

She immediately shushed him. "No, not like that, you idiot. I mean I'm jealous you got to be with him. I mean, *wow*. Those eyes. The hair. And don't get me started on that freaking body. There isn't an inch of it that shouldn't be licked."

Garrick flopped back down on the bed with a shudder. God, she was so right.

"Tell me what happened. Tell me everything."

He did.

They only lasted until the part where Rhian had Garrick's cock lodged against the back of his throat before he could hear a distinct buzzing over the phone line and his hand was flying over his cock. His brain was barely able to create speech and process the little sounds coming from Savannah while reliving what he had done with Rhian. He recalled perfectly Rhian's taste, his scent, the sounds his lover had made that night. He didn't spare a single detail.

Savannah dropped her phone when she came, but he heard her cries clearly enough to be dragged over the edge with her, his chest and abs dotted with his release.

For a long while, all he could do was breathe and stare at the ceiling. That had been almost as satisfying as being with an actual person.

Only Savannah could figure out a way to perfect phone sex.

After a cacophony of thunks and static, Savannah finally fumbled the phone back to her ear. "God, I want to see that."

"What?" he croaked.

"Rhian Savage deep-throating you," she whispered, breathless.

He groaned, shocked to feel a tingle zip through his groin. Jesus, after that orgasm, his junk should be out of commission for hours. But then he told her about how Rhian lost his voice, and it wasn't long before she came again. He told her everything. About the sex, the surprises, the long night asleep, foster care, and how they'd blown all over each other in the shower the next morning.

By her final orgasm, he'd caught up again too.

Chapter Ten

Rhian slogged out of the Moncton arena to his car, checking over his shoulder to be sure he wasn't being pursued. Three times today he'd had to dodge Garrick. He would have sworn that after five days, the guy would have given up.

It was his pride, Rhian was sure. Garrick was pissed because Rhian was avoiding him, which he could admit wasn't the most mature thing he'd ever done. But when he'd chased Garrick into his room all those nights ago, he hadn't expected...*that*.

He couldn't remember what he had been expecting, but not that.

Then Steve had shown up at Garrick's door. This was a big problem for a lot of reasons, not the least of which being that Rhian had experimented with other men while he was living with Steve. He'd never once thought Steve, or anyone else in that house, had known. But after Steve had shown up at Garrick's room, Rhian had to wonder. And worry.

Had Steve seen him chase Garrick out of the bar? Followed them?

The idea plagued Rhian and had him scanning the parking lot before pulling out into traffic. He watched the cars behind him as he drove, but quickly realized he wouldn't be able to tell if someone was tailing him. It was almost midnight and most of the cars were probably Ice Cats fans, dragging their asses home from the game.

Rhian had fled the locker room as quickly as he could, but when he pulled up in front of his crappy apartment, he wished he hadn't been in such a hurry. Going out with the guys, even if it meant avoiding Garrick, would have been better than sitting home alone.

Annoyed at his thoughts, he stalked up the stairs, his key out and almost in the lock before he realized the door was already open.

With just the tip of his key, he swung his door back, wondering if he'd somehow failed to pull it fully shut on his way out that morning. He was generally careful about those things.

Then he saw the wreckage that had once been his butt-ugly living room.

Shit.

He sighed, pulled out his phone, and dialed 911. He spoke briefly to the dispatcher, who instructed him to wait out on the curb for the cruisers to show up.

It was while he was standing there, freezing his balls off, he did either the stupidest or the bravest thing possible.

He called Garrick.

Garrick was still sitting in the locker room when his phone rang. To say he was surprised to see Rhian's number come up on the screen would be a vast understatement.

"Hello?" He didn't bother to keep the disbelief from his voice.

There was a long pause. Wouldn't it be perfect if Rhian had butt-dialed him by accident?

"Hey," Rhian said at last.

Garrick didn't say anything. After five days of being ignored, this was Rhian's show.

"I ahh…I was wondering what you're doing?"

"Right now? This very minute?" Garrick wasn't going to make it easy. Why should he?

"Yeah," Rhian said, suddenly sounding very tired.

Garrick stuck to his hard-assed guns for all of twenty seconds in the face of that dejected tone.

"You okay?"

"Yeah…no." Rhian huffed out an impatient curse. "Someone broke into my apartment. Trashed the place."

Garrick stood. "What?"

"It's okay. It's just stuff. But—"

"Where are you?" Garrick tugged on his coat.

"At my place."

Garrick narrowly resisted pointing out that his address, up until this point, was something of a state secret. Instead, he managed a polite, "What's your address?"

Rhian told him and Garrick felt an—admittedly stupid—surge of victory. He promised Rhian he'd be right there and took off for his car.

Ten minutes later, he parked behind the cruisers, their lights flashing, and searched for Rhian in front of the worn but serviceable apartment building. He climbed out of his truck when Rhian came out the front door with a duffel bag on his shoulder.

"Hey!"

Rhian veered toward him, his pleasure at seeing Garrick dimming with each step closer. Garrick would bet money Rhian was just now remembering that he'd been a total dickhead for the better part of a week.

As much as he'd like to torture Rhian about that, he'd save it for later when they had more privacy. He took the bag from Rhian when he was within reach.

"This coming with us?"

Rhian blinked. "Uhhh..."

Garrick didn't smile, though it was a struggle. "I assume you're coming back to my place tonight? To crash?" He added the last part when Rhian started to look a little panicky. Garrick was in no mood to wrestle the idiot on his front lawn, and he had no idea who would be sleeping where, in any case.

"Is that okay?" Rhian asked.

Garrick nodded once. "More than."

Rhian sighed. "Okay. Thank you. I don't want to stay here until the locks are fixed."

Garrick stowed the bag while Rhian wandered back inside. Once Garrick had locked his truck, he jogged up the walk and went in after him.

Standing in Rhian's front door, Garrick frowned at the destruction. Dishes were smashed, the shards scattered across the ancient faux-tile linoleum floor of the tiny kitchen. The living room's ubiquitous brown plaid upholstery was ripped in more places than it was intact, with cotton and foam tossed all over the cheap beige carpet. The blinds had been torn from the two windows he could see, the contents of the front hall closet—winter coats and hockey equipment—spilled from the door and were strewn across the hallway and counter that separated the kitchen from the living room.

In the thirty seconds it took to take it all in, Garrick learned two things. One, Rhian lived like a pauper and had less crap than anyone he'd ever met. Two, whoever had done this hadn't been looking for good stuff to steal, otherwise they wouldn't have smashed the TV. Whoever had done this had been *pissed*.

Rhian stood in front of his ruined entertainment center, shaking his head while the cops asked him questions. Garrick stepped into the room when the crime scene techs arrived and goosed him out of the door.

He went to Rhian's side and listened to him explain that nothing appeared to have been stolen and that with the exception of the clothes, hockey equipment, and TV, none of this stuff was his anyway.

That at least explained how Rhian had come to possess furniture that had been fashionable before he was born, if ever. It didn't explain why a guy with a decent job lived like this. Garrick had purchased his farmhouse when he'd been Rhian's age, embarking on a restoration project that had taken most of the last decade.

Rhian, on the other hand, lived like a refugee.

More questions Garrick didn't have the heart, or maybe the right, to ask.

It was late by the time the cops cut them loose and said

they'd be in touch. Garrick clapped a hand on Rhian's shoulder and steered him outside.

Rhian stopped on the sidewalk by Garrick's bumper. "I should take my own car."

Garrick pointed behind him. "You mean the one blocked in by a cruiser and the crime scene guys?"

Rhian's shoulders slumped.

Garrick almost felt sorry for him. "I'll bring you back in the morning before we go to practice," he promised.

Rhian studied Garrick. Garrick kept his face perfectly neutral.

"Okay," Rhian said at last and climbed into the truck.

Garrick allowed himself one small smile while Rhian wasn't looking and jogged around the nose of his car. He was surprised to spot Deena standing across the street, almost not recognizing her in the streetlamp's dim light. He smiled and waved, but she turned and strode away without seeing him.

He hopped into his seat and started the engine. "That was weird, huh?"

"Which part, the breaking or the entering? Or maybe the shredding?"

"No, I mean Deena."

Rhian sat up. "What?"

"I just saw her. Does she live around here?"

"Not that I've ever noticed."

They both sat quietly and digested that. Neither commented on the likelihood that she had something to do with the wreckage in Rhian's apartment.

Rhian didn't know what to think about the vandalism, or about Deena hanging out on his street. *Tonight of all nights?* It seemed like too much coincidence to him, and this kind of crazy destructive crap was right up Steve's alley.

At the risk of adding to the shit storm, he'd mention Steve

and Deena to the cops when he went in to see them tomorrow. He should have thought of Steve immediately. Why hadn't he? He was getting soft up here in the boonies, foolishly believing he'd left Chicago behind.

He rolled his head to the side to stare at Garrick's profile in the reflected light of the dashboard. He hated that Garrick had been exposed to the ugliness that used to be a staple of Rhian's life.

"I'm sorry about this," he said quietly.

"It's not a problem." Garrick glanced over at Rhian. "Actually, I'm glad you called. I was hoping to talk to you, as you may have noticed," he said dryly.

Rhian cringed. He wasn't surprised Garrick was tackling it head on but Rhian would have rather pretended it had never happened.

Well, no, that wasn't true. He'd never forget it. He just didn't want to *discuss* it.

"Why are you avoiding me, Rhi?"

Rhian grappled to come up with a reasonable explanation. He landed on the truth. "I figured it was a one-time thing and I needed time to cool off."

"So we're still friends?"

Jesus Christ, this shit was complicated. "Yes. Of course. I'm sorry." He blew out a deep breath. "I guess that's *why* I needed to cool off."

Garrick's forehead creased. "Because we're still friends?"

"Yes."

"And because it was a one-time thing," Garrick said, the barest hint of a question in his voice.

"Wasn't it?"

Garrick pursed his lips before saying, "I'm neither psychic nor willing to force you."

"What the hell does that mean?"

"It means I don't get to unilaterally decide it wasn't a one-time thing."

Garrick wants more. Rhian heart beat harder. He lifted his head. "You're in love with Savannah."

"I am."

"We're hockey players."

"We are."

"Steve showed up at your room."

"He did."

Rhian threw up his hands. He was grasping at goddamn straws and, if he were honest, it wasn't because he was trying to put Garrick off. A simple "no" would suffice there. What he was desperately trying to do was put *himself* off.

It was a bad idea. He knew it. But god help him, he wanted it anyway.

"For what it's worth," Garrick said, "I'm not worried about Steve. He doesn't know shit. Neither do the Ice Cats. We're just friends, hanging out. I promise you, I would never do anything to put you at risk."

"I know." And he did. Otherwise they wouldn't even be having this conversation.

"As to your first point, Savannah knows everything and is fine. She says hi."

"Savannah...she...*Jesus*..." Rhian trailed off. His cheeks burned. Garrick had said he'd tell her about them, but the reality of her knowing "everything" was a little embarrassing.

Desperate to move on, Rhian said the first thing that came to mind. "She sent the Bruins to look at me."

He was feeling pretty guilty about that, too. She was doing nice things to advance his career and he was fucking around with her boyfriend. *How's that for gratitude?*

One side of Garrick's mouth curled up. "She mentioned they might come by."

"She *what*?" Rhian glared at Garrick. "Why didn't you warn me?"

"As it turns out, the scout was here before I even knew about it, so it wouldn't have mattered. And I'm not sure I would have told you in any case. Savannah probably wasn't meant to tell me, and you might have been nervous."

"I could have upped my game!"

Garrick laughed. "Oh right, because you're half-assing it the rest of the time?"

Rhian didn't have a response, other than the desire to give Garrick the finger. He resisted. Barely.

"Dude," Garrick said, clearly exasperated, "relax. You've got all you need to get there. Savannah wouldn't have sent them otherwise."

Rhian's anger dissolved. He busted his ass to be the kind of player who could get picked up by the NHL, but Garrick believing it soothed something that had been jangling around in Rhian's head.

Jesus, he was getting stupider every minute he was hanging out with this guy.

Rhian slouched into his seat. "That's why Sergio was looking for me in Charlottetown. They reached out to him to ask about my contract."

"Which you very cleverly had written so that you can get released to the B's with almost no fuss."

Rhian looked at Garrick. "How'd you know that?"

Garrick opened and closed his mouth a couple times before he answered. "Because you told me?"

Rhian didn't remember doing that. It wasn't like him to tell other people his shit. He was about to question Garrick further when they crested a gentle rise and Garrick's farmhouse came into view.

The white clapboard was hardly visible from this distance, but the warm yellow lights in the windows glowed in the middle of the barren winter field. The house sat a few hundred yards back from the road, the big red barn in back a dark shadow at this time of night.

Most of the people Rhian had ever known were hockey players or foster kids. They either had never had a home or were passing through town too quickly to bother making one in whatever city they'd landed. And while most of them weren't quite as ready to bail as Rhian, no one had been settling down, either.

That had to be the reason Garrick's house freaked Rhian out. It was so warm. Comfortable. *Permanent.* It was exactly what a much younger and dumber Rhian had pictured when he'd imagined the family that had never come to take him home.

Why did I think it was a good idea to come here?

Rhian struggled to recall what the hell they'd been talking about. "Serg says they're looking at me to cover them while they've got a ton of injuries. It's probably only temporary."

"You'll make it permanent. Though the Ice Cats will be happy to work something out if you need to come back."

Rhian was flattered by Garrick's confidence, and oddly comforted by the idea he could return to Moncton— particularly given his life's goal was to make it to the NHL and never look back. "I hope you're right."

"I'm sure I am."

Rhian wanted to ask how Garrick was so certain, but he didn't want to seem like he was fishing for compliments. Besides, they were pulling into Garrick's driveway. They were almost home.

Chapter Eleven

Rhian slowly climbed the farmhouse stairs with Garrick behind him, wondering which way Rhian would go once he got to the top. Would he turn for the guest room he'd crashed in a time or two in the past, or the master suite in the opposite direction?

Garrick wasn't sure which would be better. He knew what he wanted, at a very simple and physical level. But he was also grappling with the guilt of lying to Rhian in the car.

He knew what Rhian's contract said because he'd read it. Maybe Reese shouldn't have allowed him to yet, but no one thought the deal was going to be blocked, and as the current owner, Reese had full access already.

He also knew the Ice Cats would take Rhian back because every roster report, team analysis, coach, trainer, manager, and player on the team, agreed that Rhian was the best they had. For once, the decision would be right for the team and not conflict with Garrick's innate desire to see his friend succeed.

The only thing Garrick hadn't lied about was that the Bruins would never give Rhian back once they'd seen what he could do. Oh, and the sex. He hadn't been lying about wanting whatever this thing was to be more than a one-time event.

But given everything else that had happened, it might be better if they held off on that. He was tired. Rhian looked beat. Maybe they should go to their separate corners and talk about it again in the bright light of day. Five days of the cold shoulder had been an effective reminder that even stupendous sex wasn't worth sacrificing a friendship.

Rhian stepped onto the upstairs landing and stared at the wall ahead. Garrick stopped next to him, studying his profile.

"It's up to you," Garrick said gently, though not without a pang of guilt.

Rhian looked at him. "What is this?"

It was a fair question. "Friendship?"

Rhian arched one brow.

"Okay, friendship and sex," Garrick clarified. "And before you ask, it's new to me too, so I don't know."

"Before I ask what?"

He thought about that. "I don't know."

Rhian smiled. "So you don't know the answer or the question?"

Garrick shot him a dirty look. "Fuck you."

Rhian laughed. "That's what we're talking about, isn't it?"

Just like that, arousal exploded in Garrick, draining the blood from his head and forcing it south.

"Wow," Rhian said softly.

"What?"

"Your eyes just got darker."

Savannah had mentioned they did that sometimes. Garrick shrugged, struggling to trample down his rampaging hormones.

Rhian turned to face him. "I want it..."

Hormone wrangling was now officially a lost cause.

"...but I'm nervous. Before you, I'd never been with anyone I knew."

Garrick stilled. "Ever?"

"Not really. I mean, I'd met some a time or two before we, you know, hooked up or whatever. And I saw some afterwards. But never for sex. Never more than once. Or one night. A weekend once." He shrugged. "You get the idea."

Garrick did. Rhian was hardly the first person he'd met, or been with, who could make such a claim. Though this was, to Garrick's knowledge, the first time he'd been the one to break the cycle.

"I think we have to be clear," Garrick said thoughtfully.

Rhian nodded. "Okay."

"We're friends first. All decisions take that into account and we don't do anything to fuck it up."

Rhian let go a deep breath. "Yes. Good."

"That means we err on the side of caution. Communicate expectations."

"Agreed." Rhian cocked his head. "So, what are your expectations?"

Garrick rolled his eyes. "Shit, you *would* have to ask that."

"Dude, you're the one who brought it—"

"Sorry. No, you're right." Garrick put up a hand to give himself a moment to piece his thoughts together into something intelligible. "I'm leaving for Boston in a few months. You may well get snapped up by a major team before then. Until one of those two things happens, we spend whatever time we're comfortable spending, doing whatever it is we're comfortable doing. We both have the ability to end this aspect of our friendship at any time for whatever reason. As does Savannah, to be honest. The only requirement is that any change is communicated promptly and clearly."

"In triplicate?"

"*Really*? I'm just trying to do what you—"

Rhian grabbed the front of his shirt and slammed their mouths together. Garrick fell into the kiss, threading his tongue into Rhian's mouth, the low simmer of arousal boiling over in a lip-locked instant.

It was a long, hot minute before either of them came up for air.

"Wow," Garrick said, wondering what the hell had just happened.

"It's kinda sexy when you talk like an MBA," Rhian admitted, his cheeks turning pink. He released Garrick's shirt and made a futile attempt to smooth the wrinkles with his fingers.

"Is that a yes?" Garrick asked, practically gasping from the surge of lust.

"Yes."

Rhian moaned into Garrick's mouth. Standing in the hallway, he melted under the onslaught of need as their tongues warred. His eyes slid shut when Garrick's big, warm palms clasped his face, controlling the depth and angle of the kiss.

Rhian was still nervous, but it was easy to let it go when they were doing this.

Strong arms wrapped around him and hauled his body, shoulder to knee, against Garrick. Garrick's erection was smashed against his belly and Rhian pressed forward, desperate to feel more, and almost dumped them both on their asses when their feet tangled with his bag, forgotten on the hallway floor.

Garrick steadied them with his shoulder against the wall and laughed into their kiss without stopping his assault on Rhian's mouth. It wasn't easy to maneuver when neither of them seemed willing to break apart, but they eventually managed to kick free of his bag's shoulder strap and stumble toward the bedroom door.

A glimpse of Garrick's big bed cleared Rhian's arousal-soaked brain enough for a whisper of unease to sneak in. There were things he ought to tell Garrick. More clarification might be needed. Rhian hadn't ever had a man, or anything really, in his—

Rhian gasped when his back hit the doorjamb. The wood trim tucked into the crease of his ass, hitching the seam of his jeans jammed against his balls just as Garrick's thigh wedged between his.

Rhian hummed.

This was good. Irresistibly good. Which should have been scary, but his bag was in the hall, the guest room just beyond. They'd do this, whatever it led to, then he'd go crash.

Garrick's explanation of how this thing could work made sense. Friends. Hook-ups. Temporary. The only one of those concepts Rhian wasn't well familiar with was the friendship part, and he seemed to be getting the hang of that. If they both stuck to the rules and bailed if needed, they should be okay.

It wasn't that complicated.

Garrick tore his mouth away. Rhian immediately tried to pull him back.

"Wait," Garrick gasped, catching his hands. "I refuse to do this in a doorway when the bed is right there."

Rhian no longer gave a shit *where* they did anything, as long as something was done. He staggered on rubbery legs into the middle of Garrick's room, his fingers barely brushing the buttons on his shirt before Garrick was buck naked, his clothes discarded heaps on the floor between the door and the bed.

Rhian wanted to stare at all that lovely skin and heavy cock for hours. Yanking his shirt over his head, he laughed when nimble fingers popped open his fly in the second he was blinded.

Rhian's pants were shoved to the floor while he was still trying to kick off his shoes. He would have fallen over if Garrick hadn't caught him.

"Shit, that's *still* hot," Garrick muttered as he rubbed a palm over one of Rhian's bare ass cheeks.

"What?"

"You never wear underwear."

Actually, he did sometimes, just not often. Hadn't since middle school when one particular foster mother had failed to notice he had two pairs, total. She'd had a tendency to freak if any of the kids in her care told her they needed to buy something, so Rhian had opted for more jock straps for hockey practice and learned to go commando the rest of the time.

Rhian didn't tell Garrick that, since it was pathetic crap. Instead, he enjoyed the look on Garrick's face as he stared down at Rhian's eager cock, groaning happily when Garrick's warm fingers wrapped around him and started a series of long, slow pumps.

He jumped when Garrick's lips brushed his neck, then nibbled across his Adam's apple. The air touching the wet skin Garrick left behind prickled like an icy finger running down his back. He shivered.

"You're cold," Garrick said.

Rhian lifted his head, a monumental effort. He supposed he was chilled, standing bare-assed naked in an antique farmhouse in the middle of the night in the dead of winter in New Brunswick. It seemed kind of inevitable. And unimportant.

"Here." Garrick pushed him toward the bed and folded back the thick flannel sheets and fluffy down comforter.

Rhian shivered again. The bed did look really nice and warm. He climbed in and settled on his back while Garrick pulled up the covers. Garrick smoothed the sheets under Rhian's chin, fussing with him like an old woman.

Rhian laughed. "Gee, thanks for tucking me in."

Garrick's slow smile made Rhian's heart skip in his chest. "I'll be right back."

This time his shiver had nothing to do with the temperature.

Garrick moved around the room, shutting off lights and disappearing into the bathroom. The heavy bedding, already warmed from his body heat, pressed down on Rhian. The soft pillows against his cheek smelled like Garrick.

He wasn't sure when he closed his eyes, but he smiled and peeled them open when cool air slipped beneath the covers a moment before Garrick's big, warm body bumped against his.

Garrick chuckled. "You falling asleep on me?"

"No," Rhian lied.

"Uh huh," Garrick murmured, urging him to roll over.

He did it without thinking, still hovering on the verge of sleep until Garrick's body curled around his from behind. *Oh no!* Rhian snapped fully awake, memories of their last time together crowding his mind. He thought about his bag in the hallway, his intention to sleep on his own.

The crisp click of a cap snapping closed yanked him from his spiraling anxiety. He watched Garrick's glistening hand disappear under the covers. The coarse hairs on Garrick's forearm tickled along Rhian's chest, over his hip, before his cock was enveloped in a cool, slippery fist.

Pleasure fired through him, the surge of adrenaline brought on by nerves rerouted to searing arousal. He bucked into Garrick's hand, forcing his shaft through the reservoir of lube, slicking himself to the hilt. Screwing his eyes shut, he moaned and bit his lip to help him focus on the exquisite sensations.

"You like that?" Garrick growled against his ear, his snug fist pumping steadily.

Is he fucking kidding? Rhian managed to burble something that sounded like "yes."

Garrick's hand tightened as it slid up and over the crown, his strong grip just on the good side of painfully firm. Perfect. Rhian's hips shot backward when his cock popped loose from that vise, as if shying away from the pleasure. His ass bumped against Garrick's stomach and trapped his cock between them.

Garrick hissed out a breath. "Careful."

Rhian stilled.

Garrick slipped his arm under Rhian's waist and curled around him, pinning him back against Garrick's wide chest. The thumb and index finger of Garrick's other hand wrapped around the base of Rhian's shaft, the rest of his fingers splayed to cradle Rhian's balls.

Heat streamed off Garrick's body and poured into Rhian, the power of the arms wrapped around him mesmerizing. Rhian hung suspended, his body screaming at him to move, his brain patiently waiting for Garrick to do as he wished.

Chapter Twelve

Garrick had never so completely held a lover in his hands. Literally and figuratively. Rhian's package was cradled in his palm, hard and hot. But it was the air of patient expectation, the hovering stillness awaiting his command, his any wish, that absolutely blew Garrick away.

Rhian gave himself over in response to some need they hadn't discussed and might never bother to name. It was just there, and it worked.

Slowly, Garrick stroked his fingers over the tender skin of Rhian's sac, rolling his balls, the pad of one finger slipping back to slick along the hidden seam of skin beyond. He loosened his hold around Rhian's chest, silently granting him permission to move. Rhian wriggled against the barrage of sensations Garrick thoroughly enjoyed poking and rubbing from his body—and not just because Rhian's gyrations worked Garrick's aching shaft into the valley of his ass.

Garrick loved how Rhian's body offered an endless stream of honest feedback. Garrick pumped a tight grip along the length of Rhian's cock, and Rhian's hips rotated in counterpoint. He brushed his fingers along Rhian's perineum and elicited a perfect needy sound from the back of Rhian's throat. Garrick was the conductor, Rhian his symphony. Garrick closed his eyes and absorbed every lesson to be learned about what Rhian wanted. Needed.

His fist picked up speed. Rhian's hips followed. Desire swelled, driving them on, driving them up toward crescendo. Garrick was lost to the little noises, the way his lover's eyes were screwed shut, his mouth open in a silent cry. He drowned in the sight of Rhian's ecstasy, his heart banging against his ribs at Rhian's surrender, Rhian's bliss at giving Garrick control.

Garrick was damn close to blowing until his dry shaft dragged along Rhian's burning skin one too many times and the intense friction became painful.

Groaning, he pulled his hips away, giving himself room.

"No," Rhian muttered, his hips losing rhythm to wriggle back toward Garrick.

Garrick wrapped his fist around the base of Rhian's cock and stilled, a silent command in his firm grip. Rhian immediately subsided. He whimpered when Garrick released him.

Garrick grinned and leaned over to brush his lips against Rhian's. "Can we try something?"

Rhian faltered, the flicker of unease communicated through the thousands of points where their bodies touched. His eyes slid open.

"What do you have in mind?" Rhian asked, his husky voice belied by his narrowed, nervous gaze.

Garrick had more ideas running through his head than he knew what to do with, but he discarded most of them and poured another pool of lube into his palm. Rhian's eyes tracked his movements.

Garrick slid his arms back beneath the covers and nudged Rhian's thigh. "Lift up a little."

Rhian hesitated

"It will be good. I promise."

He smiled, gratified when Rhian's knee lifted enough for Garrick to ease his slippery hand between solid, well-muscled thighs. He pulled his cock forward, groaning as he slicked his own shaft, and Rhian's thighs and perineum in the process.

"Now," he purred against Rhian's neck, "close 'em tight."

"What?"

"Trust me," he whispered.

Rhian let his leg fall, trapping Garrick's cock between his thighs.

"*Oh*," Rhian gasped. The muscles in his thighs bunched and released.

"Hmmm..." Garrick agreed, his eyes nearly crossing at the clench of hot, slippery skin. He nudged his hips forward and groaned. Wrapping one fist around Rhian's cock and pressing the other to Rhian's belly, he settled himself against his lover's back.

His next thrust fired bolts of raw pleasure up his spine, tightening his muscles until he clung to Rhian. He buried his face against Rhian's neck, his groan muffled by warm skin and soft hair.

His movements took up a rhythm. His entire existence narrowed down to the snap of his hips, the squeeze of his fingers. Rhian lay wide-eyed, his hard thighs squeezed tightly together. If Garrick closed his eyes, he could imagine their strength, how they flexed when Rhian ran, or lifted, or hell— just *walked*. He'd never guessed they would feel this good. That he would ever have an opportunity to learn their texture, their strength, so intimately.

He thrust harder and jerked Rhian's cock with punishing force and speed. Garrick's shaft slipped higher with each long drive. On the next, he slid into the hot valley between Rhian's ass and thighs and rubbed over his hole.

Rhian arched his neck and shouted unintelligibly. Garrick pressed harder, moved faster. Rhian smashed his face against the mattress and groaned. The next thrust burned along Rhian's perineum until the crown of Garrick's cock nudged hard against the back of Rhian's tight balls.

Garrick's big, strong, tough hockey-playing lover let out a sob of pure unadulterated need.

Garrick shuddered and thrust again. And again.

Rhian writhed against him, his cries hoarse. He clenched Garrick's hip with one hand, urging him on, the other scrabbling across the bed to gather a fistful of sheets to anchor them both.

"Harder. Faster," Rhian ground out, his voice hardly more than a whisper between his panting moans. His cock swelled against Garrick's palm.

Garrick wanted Rhian to unravel. To completely relinquish himself to the moment. He moved faster, squeezed tighter.

Writhing became thrashing. Rhian's legs scissored over Garrick's shaft. Muscles shifted and bulged. Garrick's plan was working perfectly, except he hadn't counted on coming so completely unglued himself.

"Rhian," he groaned. "Rhian. God please, Rhian."

Garrick couldn't stop saying his name, chanting it against his shoulder, gasping it into his neck, a ball of fire spooling in Garrick's gut, settling into his balls. Between one thrust and the next he pitched into the abyss, shocked when the first wave of release tore through him. He bit down on Rhian's shoulder and howled.

Rhian cried out, his back arching, hips jerking. Each convulsion poured Rhian's climax into Garrick's pistoning fingers and yanked another spasm out of Garrick with the clench of incredibly powerful thighs.

They lay like that, twitching, neither releasing their grip on the other, until by some unspoken agreement, they melted into the bed, Garrick half on top of Rhian.

Rhian inhaled the scent of clean cotton and Garrick from the sheets, his face buried in the mattress, his mouth hanging open while he tried to restore normal function to his brain.

It had been five minutes, at least, that he'd been lying here, enjoying Garrick's weight against his back. The aftershocks still echoed low in his body, the bite mark on his shoulder a stinging reminder of what they'd done. And how good it had been.

"Holy fuck," he muttered, trying to figure out what the hell Garrick had done to him.

He felt more than heard Garrick's laughter. He smiled, absurdly content, and closed his eyes. Just another five minutes.

His eyes popped open when Garrick shifted away. He

almost called out his objection, but retained enough sanity to keep silent. He couldn't lie here forever. He had to get his bag, go to his room, and try to sleep.

"Stay here," Garrick murmured, as if reading his mind. "I'll get something to clean us up."

Rhian nodded. Or tried to, his eyes sliding shut when Garrick pulled the covers up to his ears. Cleaning up was probably a good idea. Rhian was slicked with lube and semen from his belly to his knees, which should have been gross, but somehow just felt sexy.

Clear evidence his brain wasn't firing on all cylinders yet.

He had no idea how long he lay there before Garrick returned, peeling away the covers and wiping him down with a soft cloth. He let Garrick roll him over, move him however he needed, not bothering to wonder at the dignity of spreading his legs and letting Garrick run the soft flannel square along his perineum before pausing to rub at his anus.

"Hmmm..." His hum sounded like interest, even to his own ears. Not that he was going to be up for anything for a while, but still...

Garrick's mouth pressed gently to his, a smile against his lips. He pried his eyes open. Garrick had turned off more lights, so he couldn't see the color, but the glint of humor in Garrick's dark gaze was apparent enough.

"We'll get here eventually."

Garrick's deep voice and the press of that one finger sent shivers racing over Rhian's skin.

"But I'm going to take my time. Enjoy every step along the way. See that you do, too," he promised with another pulse against Rhian's fluttering muscles, the tip barely wedging in.

Rhian swallowed hard, staring up at Garrick without so much as blinking. He wanted that. He couldn't believe how much he wanted that.

Garrick seemed to understand, his smile widening as he leaned down and captured Rhian's mouth. Garrick's tongue danced slowly over his, deeply, as if sealing his promise.

The kiss ended and Rhian lay sprawled on this back, staring at the door. He couldn't imagine wanting to do anything *less* than he wanted to get up and leave this room. Sighing, he started to sit up.

Garrick pushed him back down. "Where are you going?" He shut off the last light, climbed into the bed, and pulled the covers over them.

Rhian opened his mouth to protest, but didn't get a word out before Garrick had manhandled him onto his side and slid his long, hard body the length of Rhian's back.

This again.

He stared hard at his bag on the dresser. He didn't remember Garrick bringing it into the room. In hindsight, he should have leaped from the bed and run like hell the minute they had finished.

Garrick's big hand rubbed over his belly, stroking the sensitive skin and soft trail of hair.

Rhian frowned. "What is this?" He'd thought he understood the answer when he'd asked the same question in the hallway earlier, but this didn't fit.

Garrick's hand paused. "Friendship?"

Rhian smiled wryly. Same answer, too. "Really?"

He half expected Garrick to say something about friendship and sex again, but Garrick surprised him.

"Yes, really." He pulled Rhian back against him, as if determined to keep him there. Garrick took up petting him again. It was distracting as all hell.

Rhian wanted to make a crack about how he didn't spoon with any of his other friends, but held his tongue. He knew the truth. There wasn't anyone else like Garrick in his life. Never had been. To pretend otherwise seemed dishonest, even if Garrick was being obtuse.

Garrick rubbed his face against Rhian's hair. "I like sleeping like this," he admitted quietly, "but if you don't or can't, then it's okay. We can stick to our own sides of the bed if you'd rather."

Rhian forced aside the pang of guilt. "What about the guest room?"

Garrick's hand stilled and Rhian instantly missed the soft caress. Silence stretched around them.

When Garrick spoke, it was in a perfectly neutral voice. "If that's what you want."

Rhian no longer knew what the fuck he wanted. "I've never... I mean..." He wasn't sure why he was trying to explain this. "I don't cuddle. With men. Or women. I've never..."

Garrick resumed his gentle stroking and Rhian felt something suspiciously like relief. It was irritating that he was so susceptible. And yet he found himself relaxing against Garrick's chest.

Which was bad. He tensed again, furiously searching for the right argument or the strength to climb from the bed.

Or not.

What the hell was wrong with him?

One moment Rhian was limp in Garrick's arms, the next he was wired tight. Rhian had cycled through whatever was gnawing at him enough times that Garrick was no longer startled by the sudden changes.

Rhian's confession didn't surprise him. That Rhian was intermittently doing a fair imitation of an oak plank was evidence enough that this wasn't easy for him. Garrick wasn't upset by Rhian's struggle so much as saddened.

Had no one ever held him?

Garrick wanted to ask. Wanted to demand to know why Rhian's mother, or father, or *someone* hadn't cherished him. But then, tales of foster care and the mess that lay in his arms were probably answer enough. All he could do was promise himself that no matter where Rhian slept that night, Garrick would accept his decision.

That didn't mean he had to cease smoothing his hand over Rhian's stomach until he decided. Or stop forcing his breaths to remain deep and even, gently rocking Rhian against his chest.

The truth was, the more Rhian battled whatever was in his head and heart, the more Garrick wanted to hold him.

Chapter Thirteen

Rhian woke with the bright rays of morning sun warming his face. A soft rumble from behind him caught his attention. He listened, half awake, and wondered at the source of the soothing noise.

When he realized it was Garrick snoring gently, his eyes snapped open.

Holy crap. *I did it again.*

As if he'd needed further proof that he was a complete idiot, the first thing his gaze landed on was the framed photograph on the bedside table. Savannah. She smiled at him, her bright green eyes dancing with laughter. And love. It was written so plainly on her face it wouldn't have been more obvious if someone had scrawled the word across her forehead with a Sharpie.

Rhian hooked one hand around the edge of the mattress and eased away from Garrick. The house was cool, the air shocking as he freed one arm and shoulder from the cocoon of down and cotton.

He almost had his foot slipped from beneath the sheets when a big hand curled around his hip and drew him back.

"Where are you going?" Garrick grumbled, his voice rusty from sleep.

The deep timbre rubbed along Rhian's skin, but it was nothing compared to the feeling of six and a half feet of warm, sleepy, naked man rolling over on top of him, pinning him face down on the bed.

Rhian's brain went blank.

It wasn't panic. Or fear. There wasn't even a hint of confusion. Just...

Peace.

He let out a deep breath and sank into the mattress.

"There you go," Garrick murmured. He slid callused hands down Rhian's arms and threaded their fingers together. "Better?"

Rhian nodded. He didn't understand what was happening, he just knew it *was* better. He would happily lie there—pressed under all this living, breathing, warm shifting weight—for hours. Days.

Soft lips and stubble trailed across the back of his neck and he hummed happily. He twitched his hips, trying to find room for his growing erection, and ended up with a steel bar wedged between the backs of his thighs.

He flashed back to the night before and hummed again. Longer and louder.

Garrick's chuckle tickled his ear. His lips teased along Rhian's neck. Sucked on his earlobe. The scrape of sharp teeth and flick of hot tongue were a welcome, if wholly unnecessary, seduction. As Garrick's mouth moved across his cheek, Rhian turned his head farther, blindly seeking a kiss.

Garrick locked onto his lips. He shifted to ease the angle their necks and lodged his cock into the valley of Rhian's ass in the process.

Rhian whimpered and sucked Garrick's tongue into his mouth as he thrust his ass up against the solid pressure of Garrick's erection. Rhian didn't know what he was doing, what he was asking for, but it felt right. Every vein and ridge of Garrick's cock electrified the sensitive skin between his cheeks.

Garrick pushed harder and Rhian whimpered again.

He didn't know how to voice his desires, wasn't even sure what they were, but he definitely wanted more.

When he shoved his ass up at Garrick again, the kiss ended with a mutual gasp. Garrick released one of Rhian's hands— Rhian didn't even consider moving it—and clutched his hip.

"Easy there," he chuckled. "You'll throw me off."

Rhian immediately subsided into the bed, his face burning.

"Oh, no you don't," Garrick muttered and captured his

mouth in another demanding kiss.

Without thought, his ass shot up and circled against Garrick's cock again. The grind was incredible, but not enough.

A flutter of nerves kicked in Rhian's chest.

Garrick, with his uncanny ability to read Rhian's mind—or maybe it was his body—sank down on top of Rhian, pressing him into the bed once more, their fingers lacing against the sheets.

The peace bled back in, washing away his anxiety.

"Stay right here," Garrick said. "Don't move."

Rhian nodded, but otherwise lay perfectly still and enjoyed the quiet in his head.

Garrick threw the covers off and knelt between Rhian's wide-spread thighs. He couldn't remember when he'd opened himself up like that, leaving himself exposed to Garrick and the cool air.

He felt vulnerable, which was funny, since he hadn't at all when Garrick had been lying on top of him, holding him down.

He cracked open one eye when Garrick leaned over and rummaged through the contents of the bedside table. Rhian couldn't see what was in the drawer, but he could guess. The nerves returned with a vengeance, not at all alleviated when Garrick came up with a fistful of objects Rhian couldn't identify.

Garrick settled on his knees between Rhian's legs and tossed whatever he'd held onto the bed by Rhian's hip. Rhian wanted desperately for Garrick to lie down on top of him again, but didn't dare ask. It was too weird, and he wasn't sure Garrick would understand. Rhian didn't understand it himself.

He jumped when Garrick put his hands on Rhian's back.

"Shhhh..." Garrick massaged his back, warming his skin, strong fingers digging at the tension knotting his muscles. Eventually, Rhian melted into the bed. Only then did Garrick stop.

Rhian realized he was a lot of damn work. Why did Garrick even bother?

"Come here," Garrick said softly.

At Garrick's urging, Rhian rolled over and sat up. Garrick wrapped a hand around the back of his neck and kissed him again.

It wasn't as effective as lying down on top of him, but the slow dance of tongues between their mouths went a long way toward erasing Rhian's worries. So did Garrick's fingers curling around his cock.

Rhian shoved both hands into Garrick's hair and kissed the fuck out of him.

Soon he was flat on his back, legs splayed around Garrick's hips, thrusting into Garrick's fist between their bellies.

Garrick was having a hard time keeping his focus with Rhian kissing him to the point of insensibility. Or maybe his head was just spinning from Rhian's ever-changing reactions.

Never in his life had he seen a person more in conflict with himself. One moment Rhian was a writhing mass of sexual need, and the next, a taut ball of worry.

Garrick was having a devil of a time keeping up, but he was starting to figure a few things out.

For one, Rhian didn't like to be held. No, wait, that wasn't right. He actually liked it quite a lot. He just wasn't very good at it. Garrick, fortunately, was available for practice.

The second thing was that while Rhian was practically panting for Garrick to do things to him, specifically *anal* things, when the overwhelming heat of passion eased off, Rhian's big brain would override his little brain and spiral into a panic.

This was a real issue for Garrick. Because *both* brains needed to consent before Garrick did anything.

Sinking further into their kiss, he tangled his tongue with Rhian's. He gloried in the squeeze of a strong hand on the back of his neck, the graceless and frantic twitch of Rhian's hips beneath him.

They'd both be more than satisfied with another vigorous

frottage, but Garrick couldn't shake the memory of that whimper, the little squeak of unadulterated need that had escaped Rhian's throat when Garrick had been grinding his cock against Rhian's tight hole.

He wanted to hear that again. He wanted to give the passionate, uninhibited lover who had made that wordless demand whatever he needed. Garrick could and would be patient.

If he moved on to what he had in mind immediately, Rhian would freeze up. He'd like to insist Rhian trust him, but that was stupid. And wrong. Not just because trust was something Rhian had to give freely, but because Garrick hadn't earned it. He'd been lying to Rhian. To everyone on the team, actually, but it only mattered here. Now.

Garrick broke the kiss. "I have something I have to tell you."

Rhian's eyes opened slowly, his gaze vague. Trusting.

It punched Garrick right in the gut, leaving him speechless.

Rhian quirked one eyebrow. His lips were swollen and red, his cheeks pink.

Words simply fell out of Garrick's mouth. "God, you're beautiful."

Rhian blinked.

Garrick shifted away, trying to give himself room to think. He slid down Rhian's body and Rhian lifted his knees higher, tilting his hips so Garrick's junk ended up back where it had started—against Rhian's ass.

Rhian inhaled sharply and wriggled against Garrick's shaft. *"Do something."*

Need roared through Garrick. "What are you asking for?" he gasped. He needed to hear Rhian say it.

Rhian stared up at him with breathtaking trust. "Anything."

Wow. Garrick sucked in a couple deep breaths, trying to slow his heart rate without success. He pulled away from Rhian and sat up on his knees, watching for the panic to return.

It didn't. There was no fear. No change. Rhian lay spread before him, patiently waiting for Garrick to do as he pleased.

He almost blew then and there. He reached for the lube with an unsteady hand and held it where Rhian could see.

There. Garrick knew the moment Rhian's brain came back online.

"We're not going to fuck," Garrick said softly, skimming his palm up one of Rhian's thighs. "Not today. Not nearly enough time today. And not until you're ready."

He thought Rhian might protest and was pleased when he didn't.

He popped the cap on the lube and slicked one finger, studying every nuance of Rhian's expression as he gently stroked across Rhian's tightly puckered muscles, teasing over his anus in a series of slow circles.

Rhian's mouth fell open. His eyes dilated until the blue was lost to abject arousal.

Garrick smiled. Rhian wasn't afraid of anal play, he was nervous about anal *sex*. Garrick filed that away, more confident that this morning's adventure would be well within Rhian's comfort zone.

Garrick pressed the tip of his finger against the tight ring and wriggled it. The muscles gave easily, answer enough, but he wanted to hear the words.

"Is this okay?"

"Yes," Rhian said on a gasp.

Garrick smiled and with a gentle twist, sank his finger in to the first knuckle.

"Oh fuck, Garrick!"

The astonished ecstasy on Rhian's face mesmerized him. Nearly equally seductive was the sight of his finger slowly working its way into Rhian's hot, clinging body.

Garrick's gaze flicked back and forth, gauging Rhian's reaction, his body's accommodation as Garrick pumped his finger in and out, pressing against the velvet walls, stretching little by little. His added lube, liberally, until Rhian was slicked inside and out, his long groans and heavy pants timed with the rhythm of Garrick's thrusts.

He slipped in a second finger.

Rhian's back arched off the bed, his hands fisting in the sheets, his head thrown back.

Garrick spread his fingers and a low, fierce whimper tore from Rhian's throat.

There it is.

Garrick smiled and groped for the other item he'd fished from the drawer. At last his fingers curled around the new, smallish butt-plug. It was no wider than one and a half of his fingers and perfectly curved to nail Rhian's prostate.

He pulled his fingers from Rhian's ass and slipped the plug into place.

Rhian's groan of disappointment ended with a sharp grunt. His eyes snapped open and he sat up, grabbing Garrick's arms to hold himself steady.

"What the fuck is that?"

Rhian tried to make sense of the sensations storming his body. His ass felt full, but not as much as when Garrick had slid his fingers in and spread them. Now there was a crazy heaviness which it took Rhian some time to recognize as steady pressure on his prostate.

He blinked and looked up at Garrick.

"You okay?" Garrick smiled. He appeared quite pleased with himself.

Rhian nodded slowly. Even that miniscule shifting of his weight sent lightning bolts firing through his body.

Holy crap, he needed to come so badly, he thought he might suffer permanent damage if he didn't do it soon. Garrick didn't look much better off, the head of his erection flushed a deep scarlet that appeared almost painful.

Rhian fell back on the bed, momentarily blinded by the shockwaves roaring through him. He licked his lips. "Come here," he said, his voice hoarse.

Garrick lifted one brow. Generally he was the one in charge—and Rhian had no complaints about that whatsoever—but Rhian was at the end of his rope. He knew what he wanted and he wanted it *now*.

Hell, he'd beg for it. "*Please.*"

He grabbed Garrick's thigh and spun him so that they were going in opposite directions.

Garrick looked at him over his shoulder. "You sure?"

Was he fucking *ever*. With another tug, Garrick straddled his head, his mouth hovering above Rhian's erection, hot breath rushing over the excruciatingly sensitive head.

Rhian arched his neck and, using one hand to guide him, slid Garrick's cock all the way down his throat.

Garrick gripped one of Rhian's thighs painfully hard. "Oh Jesus Christ, Rhian! Oh, fuck! Oh god! Ohshitshitshit!"

Rhian couldn't smile or laugh, but a bubble of pure joy worked its way through his system, joined by surging endorphins as he swallowed around the thick shaft blocking his airway.

"*Rhian!*"

He used both hands to ease Garrick back, sucking in air before he stretched his neck and pulling Garrick down for another deep thrust into his throat.

Garrick trembled above him, crying out his pleasure. He wrapped his hands around Rhian's thighs, lifting and spreading them wide, until Rhian's feet were planted on the mattress and his junk was on display. It felt shameless and wicked. And perfect.

Then Garrick clutched Rhian's hips and bore him down into the mattress with his full weight.

Rhian fell back to the bed, Garrick's cock springing free from his lips. "Oh! Fuck. Oh—"

Fuck. The plug shifted, doing unspeakable things deep in his ass. The pressure on Rhian's prostate was amazing. Intense. As if that wasn't enough, Garrick chose that moment to slip the head of Rhian's cock past his soft lips and into the furnace of his mouth. His velvet tongue bathed the crown, whisking away the constant ooze of pre-come.

Then he bounced Rhian's ass on the bed again.

Rhian roared.

Garrick took up a steady rhythm of shoving Rhian's plug-jammed ass against the mattress before sucking his cock into his wicked mouth as Rhian bounced back up.

"Oh Jesus, *Garrick.*"

He couldn't catch his breath. Couldn't think. He needed a distraction. Something to keep him from coming in the first ten seconds. He threw his elbows out and shoved Garrick's knees apart until Garrick's cock was pressed to his lips.

He didn't dare try to take Garrick deep, afraid he'd choke or bite when another surge of pleasure swelled up out of his ass. Instead he licked the shaft once, twice, slicking it for his hand before nudging Garrick forward and sucking the tender skin of his sac into his mouth.

Garrick's muffled groan vibrated up Rhian's cock and into his gut.

Rhian pumped his hand along Garrick's shaft in time to his bouncing on the bed. He quickly worked a finger into his mouth, wetting it thoroughly, then dragged the tip up the seam of Garrick's perineum until he found the tight knot of muscle protecting Garrick's ass.

Garrick froze. Rhian's cock slipped from his mouth.

Shit.

Rhian wanted to growl, furious with himself. He'd killed the moment.

Garrick sucked in a deep breath. "Are you going to do it?"

Rhian stopped pulling his hand away. "Do you want me to?"

"Fuck. *Yes.*"

Rhian tapped against Garrick's hole one, twice, almost laughing at how Garrick's entire body twitched with each contact. Then Rhian twisted his finger and groaned when it slipped into Garrick's tight, hot ass. Garrick groaned, too. He tossed something onto the bed beside Rhian's head.

The lube. Rhian smiled.

Seconds later, his slick finger sank into Garrick to the hilt. Holy fuck, it felt amazing. So tight. So *hot.*

Garrick resumed his torture of bounce and suck with a vengeance. Rhian could barely function while Garrick pounded his ass down on the bed, no longer letting Rhian's cock slip from his lips, but running his tongue along it over and over.

Rhian shoved his finger farther into Garrick's ass and thumped Garrick's prostate soundly.

Garrick's long moan bowed Rhian's spine right off the bed. He desperately tried to stave off his orgasm, clenching his ass and realizing too late that with the plug in, it had the opposite effect.

He shoved a second finger in with the first.

Garrick threw back his head and howled Rhian's name, his full weight grinding Rhian's ass down on the bed. The arch of Rhian's spine planted the plug firmly into the mattress and shoved it high in his ass. Ecstasy burned through his veins, lighting him up until his legs shook, his eyes watered, and his balls clenched up tight. From one breath to the next, his climax exploded outward.

Never in his life had he made a sound like the one that flew from his mouth. His nose buried against Garrick's balls, he cried out, his fist clamping down on Garrick's shaft as the waves racked him.

Garrick shuddered above him, groaning his name as spots of wet heat landed across Rhian's chest and abs.

Chapter Fourteen

Garrick drove out of the arena parking lot three nights later and wondered if he'd been wrong. Again. Maybe persuading Rhian into more than a one-time thing had been a bad idea. Maybe being with him at all was a mistake.

Not that he hadn't loved every damn minute, but if the cost was days of Rhian avoiding him, it wasn't worth it. Rhian struggled with so much about their relationship—even the friendship. Garrick feared he was just making it worse.

At least the past few days hadn't been as bad as last time. Rhian still sat with him at practice and meetings, their lockers were back to being next to each other even when they'd traveled to Fredericton yesterday. They still hung out with their friends together. Or at least as much as Garrick could these days.

But at the end of each day, Rhian had told him he needed to go home, to be alone, and Garrick hated the look in his eyes when he said it.

It was supposed to be *fun,* damn it. Not scary.

To top it all off, guilt gnawed at Garrick. If Rhian would agree to spend ten minutes alone with him, Garrick would tell him everything. And then it probably wouldn't matter how much he wanted Rhian. Rhian would know Garrick had been lying to him.

If he had learned nothing else, he knew how rare trust was for Rhian. The longer Garrick waited to confess, the bigger it grew in his mind. The more he feared Rhian's reaction.

He wouldn't be able to tell Rhian tonight either. Garrick had a meeting with Rupert—who was *finally* in town—and Reese at his farmhouse. Rupert would start as the full-time manager tomorrow, and they had a lot to discuss, not the least of which was the roster. With a heavy heart, Garrick had accepted that Justin needed to be cut loose.

Another betrayal for which he could only hope to be forgiven.

Sighing, he pulled onto the highway headed out of town. He'd barely gotten up to full speed when his phone rang.

Rhian stood in the bitterly cold wind of the arena parking lot and frowned at his car sitting on the pavement. Literally. All four tires had been slashed, leaving his rims firmly planted on the ground with black rubber pancakes pinched beneath them.

Shit.

He fished the card for the detective assigned to the break-in at his apartment from his wallet and dialed the number. It wasn't until he was relating the details of this latest fiasco that he noticed a note tucked under his windshield wiper.

He plucked it loose as he hung up the phone, having assured the detective he would wait for the police to arrive. It was a simple piece of white lined paper torn from a spiral notebook. The handwriting was neat and unremarkable. The message, terrifying.

$5000 OR WE TELL THE PRESS, THE BRUINS, AND YOUR FANCY AGENT YOU'RE A FAGGOT.

There followed instructions to leave an envelope of small bills taped under a bench at the local shopping plaza tomorrow.

Rhian was hardly aware he'd dialed his phone again until Garrick's voice was in his ear.

"Rhian? Are you okay?"

Garrick probably assumed he would only call if the shit hit the fan, and he was right.

I'm such a jerk.

Rhian wished, not for the first time, he could get over the fear that hounded him when he was faced with his decisions in the bright light of day. When he didn't have Garrick's arms around him and his lips distracting him.

"Rhian?"

Fear or no fear, he couldn't deny the truth. "I need you."

"Where?"

No hesitation. No explanation needed. The squeal of tires was loud over the phone.

"Garrick, be careful."

"Where are you?"

Rhian told him, so fucking relieved Garrick was coming back. Only after he hung up did it occur to him that the best response to someone trying to out you was probably not to have your lover come riding in like a knight in shining armor.

He scanned the parking lot. Was he being watched?

Dave and Chris were cutting across the rows toward their cars. Rhian waved them over.

"What the fuck!" Dave exclaimed when they arrived at Rhian's side and saw what was left of Rhian's tires.

Rhian relaxed a little, glad to have some company—particularly teammates who had been in the arena with him when this happened, so they couldn't possibly be responsible. He hated the cynical thought, a terrible reminder of the constant suspicion he'd honed while living in the group homes.

He'd shaken free of so much of that, damn it, and now this ugly shit. He searched the parking lot again.

Chris cocked his head. "What are you looking for?"

Rhian shrugged.

Dave caught on. "Chris, go see if anybody is over there." He pointed at the rows between them and the fence. "I'll look this way." He took off in the opposite direction.

Rhian wanted to call them back, unwilling to risk their safety, and yet was so damn grateful for their support he could feel an alarming sting in the back of his eyes.

Holy Jesus, he needed more sleep. He'd spent the last three night tossing and turning, hardly getting a wink. He hadn't had a good night's sleep since...

Well, whatever. He wasn't going to think about that right

now.

A police cruiser pulled into the lot, lights flashing, and Garrick's SUV tore in right behind it. Rhian flagged down the officers while Garrick's truck rocked to a stop in the first available spot. He leaped from his car and ran toward Rhian.

For a moment, Rhian was afraid Garrick was going to do something crazy like crash right into him and hold on.

Or maybe that was just wishful thinking.

Rhian turned to the officers. Garrick came to stand at Rhian's shoulder without saying a word. The barest brush of Garrick's hand against his hip settled Rhian's nerves.

He assured the cops he knew nothing more than when they'd met at his apartment, ignoring the blackmail note burning a hole in his pocket.

The police went to talk to Dave and Chris. As soon as they were out of earshot, Garrick's hand came to rest on his back.

"Are you okay?"

Rhian quickly stepped away and turned to face him.

"It's not what you think," Rhian said, desperate to wipe the hurt from Garrick's face. "We need to talk."

How the hell was he going to tell Garrick about the note? Christ, what if there was proof? Only one other person could be in any pictures or, god forbid, video.

What the fuck have we done?

Garrick glanced at his watch and swore. "I have to get home. Will you come with me? Please."

Rhian shifted uncomfortably. He needed to talk to Garrick alone, but another night at the farmhouse might draw him deeper into whatever this thing was between them.

Friendship. Sex. These didn't feel like the right words anymore, but Rhian couldn't come up with better ones. All he had was the burning desire to run away and the overwhelming need to get as close to Garrick as he possibly could.

Jesus, he was such a fuck-up.

Garrick cocked his head, waiting for an answer.

"Didn't you have plans tonight?" Rhian hedged.

"I do. I'm meeting some people at the house, but you can come with me. I'll explain on the way home."

That sounded less intimidating than going home with him alone. "Okay."

Once he agreed, Rhian felt nothing but relief. And excitement. Which was stupid, but par for the course these days. Even in his most freaked-out moments, the low hum of desire had never once deserted him. He wanted this man to the point of distraction.

Of course, once he dropped the bomb about the blackmail, there was a very good chance Rhian would be delivered back to his apartment with all possible haste.

He checked in with the officers again while Garrick called a friend who owned a garage to come get Rhian's car. Four new tires would be pricey, especially on top of replacing the stuff that had been ruined during the break-in. It probably said something about him that the first thing he'd done was order a new TV.

Garrick ended his call and immediately dialed another number.

Rhian wondered when he'd decided a TV would make his sad little space a home. And when had he started to want that anyway?

"Just hang tight. I'll be there as soon as I can," Garrick said quietly into his phone. He glanced at Chris standing a few feet away and turned his back, stepping closer to Rhian. "Okay, thanks. Sorry for the delay. I'll explain when I get there."

Garrick hung up.

"I'm sorry I screwed up your plans for tonight."

"This is more important."

Their gazes tangled and held, Garrick's warm brown eyes soothing something deep inside Rhian. His fears, the knots of tension that had lived in his gut since they'd last been alone, eased. At that moment, all he wanted was to go somewhere private where Garrick could lie down on top of him.

Garrick pulled his SUV out onto the highway with a white-knuckled grip on the steering wheel.

It was time for him to confess.

"Rhi—"

"Gar—"

They laughed and fell silent again.

Rhian turned to him. "You go first."

Great.

Garrick struggled to find a way to soften the news, or at least the delivery. He'd like to have finessed this one into the net, but it was going to be a slapshot.

"I own the Ice Cats."

"What?"

"Actually, I only own one quarter of the Ice Cats." The clarification hardly mattered, but he'd try anything.

"*What?*"

Garrick's heart sank. He considered pulling over so he could grab hold of Rhian and try to explain that he'd made a huge fucking mistake. But then, his touch might not be welcomed. And goddamn Reese and Rupert were waiting at the house—thus why he was doing this at sixty miles per hour and not once they were home.

When Rhian said nothing, Garrick laid his hand over Rhian's fist on the center console. Rhian whipped his arm away, leaving Garrick to stare out at the empty highway with what felt like a boulder lodged in his chest.

Chapter Fifteen

Rhian tried to wrap his head around what Garrick had just told him. He blurted out the first clear thought that landed. "Holy fuck, you're my boss."

"I am not."

Rhian glared at the stupid man. "Yes, you are. You can sign me, terminate me, trade me, promote me. You name it. Jesus fucking Christ, Garrick, I thought you were my *friend*."

His voice echoed in the small cab.

Garrick's Adam's apple bobbed. His voice was low and rough. "God, Rhian. I *am* your friend."

Rhian turned away when Garrick looked at him.

Goddamn him.

Rhian barely had a handle on how this shit was supposed to work, but he knew this wasn't right. He'd trusted Garrick. Told him...well, told him more than he'd ever intended. More than he'd told anyone else.

Goddamn him.

"I'm not supposed to tell anyone, Rhian. Not until the deal is finalized."

"I bet Savannah knows." He wished he could take the words back the second they left his mouth.

Garrick's silence was answer enough. Rhian didn't expect any further explanation. It wasn't as though he'd had any illusions about what this was between them.

"She knows because she's the one who found the other buyers," Garrick said at last.

That got Rhian's attention.

"There are four partners," Garrick explained. "Me, Callum Morrison, Duncan Morrison, and Edwin Lamont. No one is supposed to know that. No one does know it except some lawyers, the league, the partners, Rupert Smythe, Savannah, and now you."

Callum and Duncan Morrison were NHL super-stars. "Savannah Morrison," he muttered, piecing it together.

Garrick smiled a little. "Her brothers."

On top of everything else, learning his friend was the sister of two of his heroes seemed almost trivial.

Garrick owns the Ice Cats?

Two months ago the team had been up for sale and there had been talk they'd be disbanded when the only bidder had been shipped off to prison. Then some anonymous partners had gone in with the old owner and saved the team. Edwin Lamont had been the one threatening to shut them down, but somehow he'd been convinced to stick around and reinvest. Convinced, it seemed, by…*Garrick?*

Shit. Without the new investors, Rhian had been facing the very real possibility of scrambling to find a new team. Garrick had saved his bacon. Everyone's fucking bacon.

Rhian rubbed his fingers against his temple. He couldn't decide if he wanted to punch Garrick in the nose or kiss him.

Garrick turned into his driveway, his headlights illuminating the front porch where Rupert Smythe stood with someone Rhian didn't recognize.

"Who's with Smythe?"

"Errr… that's Reese."

A host of questions popped into Rhian's head. He'd been as shocked as the rest of the team when it was announced Rupert was taking over when Mark left. For Christ's sake, the man appeared to be terrified of his own shadow. Had Garrick been part of this crazy decision?

"Is this Reese guy going to help Rupert manage the team?"

"Rupert will be fine." He said it like he was determined to make it true.

"That's why you're retiring. Because you bought the team." It wasn't really a question, more like spouting out conclusions as the puzzle pieces fell into place.

Garrick shook his head. "I'd be retiring regardless. Arthritis in my hip. And I don't intend to be away from Savannah for another season."

Garrick had a bad hip?

Rhian had thought he knew this man. Turned out, he didn't know shit. God, he was an idiot. He *knew* better. Knew not to let his guard down, but like a fool, he'd trusted Garrick, and done...well, just thinking about what they'd done together made heat crawl up his neck.

He couldn't change that, so he'd focus on what he knew now. Garrick was his boss and was leaving to be with Savannah.

What more information did he need, really?

As soon as they came to a stop, he got out of the truck and threw the door shut.

Garrick jolted when the door slammed with a loud crack. That had gone as badly as he'd feared it would. Worse, even.

He had to fix this. He'd beg for forgiveness. Do whatever he had to do to convince Rhian he *was* his friend. He had to erase that look from Rhian's eyes.

He jumped from the truck. "Rhian. Wait."

Rhian stopped in the middle of the walkway to the front porch but didn't turn around.

Garrick ran to his side. "Please, listen to me."

"I trusted you."

Garrick staggered back at the hurt packed into those three little words.

Rhian didn't spare him a glance. He jogged up the porch stairs and nodded to the men watching them with avid interest.

Garrick followed and unlocked his door on autopilot, while his mind cast around for a solution. He needed to talk to Rhian. He needed to meet with Reese and Rupert, and get them the fuck out of his house as quickly as possible. Christ on a crutch, he wanted to explode from being pulled in so many directions.

Rhian strode into the front hall and stopped, looking between the stairs and the living room, clearly not certain where to go.

Garrick spoke without thinking. "Go on up to bed. I'll come up as soon as I can."

The words rang like a bell on a clear night, hanging in the air around them.

God, and he'd thought Rhian had looked betrayed before? Garrick's heart broke. He'd just done the unthinkable. He'd outed Rhian.

Rhian's eyes darted to the door. Garrick barely repressed the urge to tackle Rhian to the floor to keep him from leaving.

He grabbed Rhian's arm and dragged him away from Reese and Rupert. "I'm sorry. I'm so sorry," he whispered. "But I swear to god, Rhian, they can be trusted. Please believe me. You don't have to be afraid."

Rhian just stood there, letting Garrick shake his arm as the words bounced off him.

At last, Rhian blinked.

When Garrick opened his mouth to apologize again, Rhian shook his head slowly in that way Garrick's grandmother used to do to tell him just how horribly disappointed she was in him, then yanked his arm free.

Garrick figured Rhian might try to hike the ten miles back to Moncton in the dead of night, but he turned and climbed up the stairs without another word for anyone.

Jesus Christ, I really fucked it up this time. Garrick scrubbed his hands over his face while he listened to the creak of his stairs and the hallway above.

He had barely registered that Rhian was walking toward the master bedroom when he was slammed back against the wall.

"You're fucking cheating on Savannah?" Reese was right in

his face, an impressive effort given that Garrick was a good six inches taller. Rupert stood at Reese's back, his face flushed with anger.

Garrick met Reese's glare calmly. "No."

"Don't bullshit me, Garrick," Reese snarled. "Savannah's been out of town, what, *a month*? And you can't keep it in your fucking pants? She deserves better. And what kind of self-destructive bullshit are you into that you'd fuck around on the sister of your new business partners? Are you *trying* to fucking ruin us?"

Garrick could shove Reese clear across the room and possibly into the next, via the wall, with little effort. God help him, one good growl would probably reduce Rupert to terror. He didn't have the will or the energy to do either. In fact, he respected Reese for leaping to Savannah's defense.

He slumped back against the wall and closed his eyes. "It was her idea."

No one moved. He cracked his eyes back open in time to see Rupert and Reese exchange a look before Reese gave him a narrow-eyed stare. "Explain."

Garrick wondered idly if he'd be able to keep one fucking secret to himself tonight. Probably not. As one quarter owner of the Ice Cats and the man who'd taken a huge risk on Garrick, Edwin Reese Lamont had a right to know.

With a long sigh, he told them about his deal with Savannah.

Reese let go of his shirt sometime around his pink-cheeked admission that he was required to tell her everything. When he was finished, he left them to mull over his goddamn not-so-private life while he went to make coffee.

They wandered into the kitchen a few minutes later.

Garrick leaned back against the counter and crossed his arms over his chest. "Anything else you want to know?"

Reese ran a hand through his hair and smiled sheepishly. "Does she have a sister?"

Garrick shot a look at Rupert, who was laughing until he saw Garrick's expression.

Rupert rolled his eyes. "Don't look at me." He gestured at Reese. "The damn fool insists on being straight in spite of my best efforts to convince him of what he's missing."

Huh. Garrick had assumed they were both gay. And *together*.

"It's true." Reese said, sounding for all the world like he regretted being a disappointment to Rupert.

Garrick was amazed to feel his lips twitch.

While he poured the coffee, Reese and Rupert turned their attention to the paperwork he'd left spread out across his kitchen table. As usual, Rupert spouted off the numbers and projections from his head, hardly referring to any of the reports. Reese, meanwhile, questioned every proposal and conclusion, entrenched in his role of devil's advocate. For their first few meetings this had driven Garrick crazy. Now, god help him, he was starting to enjoy it.

It wasn't long before the roster made it to the top of the agenda and Garrick proposed trading Justin for a player out of Halifax who would better fill out their lines.

He got no arguments—*none,* goddamn it—and they decided to proceed. Garrick carefully arranged his face in his most professional and neutral expression and doggedly ignored the way Reese kept looking at him like he was waiting for him to crack. He wasn't going to crack. Trading Justin was the right thing to do for the team. That Reese didn't pick at it meant they'd already figured this out and had been waiting for him to get the balls together to do it.

Garrick refused to be embarrassed.

They'd been sitting together for a few hours when Reese started pushing to wrap things up. Garrick had assumed they'd be working late into the night, given how much they had to catch up on. Unfortunately, every time they spoke about Rupert assuming his new duties tomorrow, he got paler and paler—and he was an Englishman, for crying out loud. He'd started out the color of milk.

Garrick hoped like hell Rupert got his shit together fast. He knew Rupert could do the job. He just needed to man the fuck up.

Garrick kept that and a host of other, similar suggestions to himself.

Reese, on the other hand, looked like he was gagging on the need to give Rupert an earful the minute they were alone. Garrick was happy to leave that job to him.

As they pulled on their coats, Garrick put his hand on Reese's arm. "Can I tell Rhian?"

"Tell him what?"

"Who you really are."

Reese thought about it, glancing at Rupert, who nodded. "If you trust him."

"I do."

"I'm not sure he's very happy with you right now. Is that going to be a problem?"

"No. He's a good man. He can be trusted."

Reese sent Garrick a pitying look. "I bet you wish you'd thought of that before tonight."

"Yeah."

"Fine, tell him. Please make him understand that he needs to keep it to himself."

"He will."

Reese nodded, and with a final goodnight, he and Rupert went out to their waiting car.

Garrick locked the door, straightened up the kitchen, and shut off the lights downstairs. He texted Savannah that he loved her and stared at his phone, hoping for a response in spite of the late hour. None came.

With a deep, fortifying breath, he quit stalling and trudged up the stairs to his room.

Chapter Sixteen

When Rhian had fled up the stairs earlier, he'd marched straight to Garrick's room with every intention of sitting in the chair and waiting until Garrick came to find him. Eventually, though, the late hour and his long day caught up with him. He'd contemplated hauling his carcass down the hall to the guest room, but he was afraid Garrick would avoid the conversation until morning.

They needed to talk *tonight*.

That was the only reason he was dead asleep on top of Garrick's comforter, fully clothed beneath the soft quilt that had been folded over the foot of the bed, his head buried in pillows that smelled comfortingly of Garrick's shampoo.

He woke when Garrick sat on the bed beside him.

"Am I welcome?" Garrick said quietly.

Rhian rolled onto his back and sighed. "It's your bed."

Garrick nodded, but didn't make a move to get up or lie down. "I'm really sorry, Rhian."

Rhian believed him, he just wasn't sure it made any goddamn difference. They were up to their asses in alligators and Garrick didn't even know the half of it yet.

"Out of curiosity, which part are you apologizing for? Not telling me that you bought the team? Or for outing us?"

"Jesus. *Both*. Look, I should have told you about the Ice Cats. I wanted to. If I could go back, I would. You have to know I trust you. I just didn't realize how hard it would be."

"Owning the team?"

"No, not being one of the guys anymore."

"You're still one of the guys, Garrick."

Garrick shook his head. "No, you were right. I'm the boss. One of them, anyway. I've even been doing Mark's job for a while, actually. Until Rupert could get here and take over."

Rhian recalled the look on Rupert's face when Garrick had made it glaringly obvious Rhian was supposed to tuck himself into Garrick's bed to wait for him. "Jesus, Garrick. Rupert Smythe is our manager. I work for him—*too*."

Rhian shoved the quilt aside, but Garrick's hand on his arm stopped him from sitting up.

"Rupert is not going to tell anyone about us."

"Why not?"

"In addition to being a decent guy who wouldn't do shit like that, he's gay. I'm going to go out on a limb and say that probably makes him sensitive to the issue."

That *was* marginally reassuring. "And what about the other guy? Who the hell was that?"

Garrick smiled. "That's Reese."

"Who?"

"Edwin Reese Lamont."

Rhian's mouth fell open. "*That's* Edwin Lamont?"

Garrick chuckled. "Yeah, I had the same reaction."

"I thought he was—"

"Older? Uglier?" Garrick laughed and the sound tugged a smile from Rhian.

He lay there, stunned, as Garrick explained that Reese chose to keep his identity a secret. Reese relied on the assumption that Edwin Lamont was some reclusive old dude who never left his estate on Nova Scotia so he could move freely in public.

Rhian could tell by the way Garrick spoke about both Reese and Rupert that they were his friends. He trusted them. It helped Rhian relax a little.

What really eased his mind, though, was that Rhian knew things about both Rupert and Reese that they didn't want made public any more than Rhian did his love life. Mercenary? Yes. But also realistic. If tonight had proved nothing else, Rhian needed to get back to being realistic.

"There's more," Garrick said quietly.

Rhian's stomach churned. This time Garrick didn't stop him from sitting up. "What?"

"We're trading Justin. Tomorrow."

Rhian was sorry to hear that. Justin was a good man and would be missed. None of that explained the utter misery on Garrick's face.

"That's too bad," Rhian said slowly.

"I understand if you're angry."

Rhian was definitely missing something. "Why would I be angry?"

Garrick frowned. "Don't you get it?"

Rhian shook his head. "I guess I don't."

"It was my decision." Garrick swallowed hard. When he spoke again, his voice was husky. "*I* did it."

Rhian stared, horrified, at the sheen in Garrick's eyes. He reached for Garrick, but he shied away and tried to stand up.

Oh, hell no.

He grabbed Garrick's arm and forcibly hauled his unwilling friend against his chest. Rhian didn't know what the fuck he was doing, having not actually hugged someone in...well, maybe ever. He kept on doing it anyway.

It didn't matter that Justin was leaving. Or that Rhian didn't know why. Garrick wouldn't do it unless it was the right thing to do. Just like Garrick wouldn't run the team into the ground, jeopardizing the rest of the players and staff, just because what had to be done hurt like hell.

With gut-churning dismay, Rhian accepted that he *did* know Garrick. That no matter what he'd learned today, he trusted him. Implicitly.

It was stupid and reckless and probably going to cost him, but Rhian didn't pretend he could change it.

He pulled Garrick closer.

Garrick pressed his face against his neck, his arms curling around Rhian's back. With a deep sigh, Garrick melted against him.

Something loosened in Rhian's chest.

Comfort. He'd given Garrick comfort, and he felt like a fucking hero.

He buried his face in Garrick's hair, inhaling the clean and familiar scent. This felt good. It felt real. It felt like…

Rhian yanked his arms from around Garrick and fell back onto the bed. "I—"

The words choked off in his throat.

I love you.

Holy fucking shit. This couldn't be right. *It couldn't.*

He bolted upright, his legs pedaling until his back slammed against the headboard.

"Rhian?"

Garrick's worried voice called to him through his spiraling panic. He looked at his friend, his lover, and shook his head frantically, flailing for an explanation for his behavior. For a reason to escape.

Fuck reason.

Leaping to his feet on the mattress, he made it one step toward the door before Garrick hooked his legs and threw him down on the bed.

His mind went blank. He couldn't draw enough air to scream. He thrashed, desperate to fight his way out. Away. He battled against Garrick's hold.

"Rhian! *Rhian!*"

He had to get away. Back to his apartment. Lock himself in. Be safe.

Not like this. He couldn't stand to be like *this.*

Heart pounding as if he'd sprinted for miles, he kept fighting. Garrick's breath wheezed past Rhian's ear when his elbow slammed into Garrick's chest. He almost broke free.

Then he was flying, the world spinning as he was lifted right off the bed and flipped face down.

He howled with frustration and terror, his cry cut off when something huge and warm crashed down on his back and smashed him into the mattress. *Garrick.* He let out another hoarse shout and heaved upwards to throw the weight off. Garrick yanked his arms out from him and they slammed down onto the bed together. Powerful fingers threaded through his, stilling his hands.

He gasped. Gasped again, drawing more air this time.

At last he heard a voice.

"Breathe, baby. You have to breathe."

He did. Once. Twice. The pain in his chest easing. The chaos in his brain cleared enough that he could focus on Garrick's voice. His scent. His warm weight.

Shuddering, Rhian sank deep into the cool cotton beneath them. Defeated.

"You're safe, Rhian. I promise. I won't let anything happen to you."

Too late. It already has.

Garrick struggled to regulate his breathing as he whispered into Rhian's ear, the soft words rushing from him until the hard muscles beneath him went lax.

Holy Christ, what the hell was that?

He lay still, not sparing Rhian an ounce of his weight, and blinked against the sting in his eyes. When Rhian's eyes finally fluttered shut, Garrick pressed his damp cheeks to the soft cotton of Rhian's shirt.

He'd tackled and pinned Rhian to the bed because he'd been afraid his friend would hurt himself. He stayed because it seemed to help. He didn't know why. Or how. It didn't matter, as long as it worked.

Garrick never wanted to see terror like that on Rhian's face again. Ever. Wide, sightless blue eyes with pin-prick pupils would haunt him for the rest of his life.

Neither of them moved nor spoke for a long time. Garrick would have remained there all night if needed, but eventually Rhian shifted beneath him.

Garrick pressed his cheek to Rhian's and rubbed against the coarse stubble, soothing himself.

"Better?"

Rhian nodded.

Garrick had zero experience with panic attacks, but he was sure that's what had just happened. Rhian seemed calm now, but Garrick worried whatever had possessed Rhian still simmered beneath the surface.

"Will you be okay if I get up?"

Garrick felt Rhian take some deep breaths and waited. Eventually, Rhian nodded.

Garrick eased himself off Rhian and rolled to lie beside him on the bed.

"Are you okay?"

The tiny shake of Rhian's head was heartbreaking.

"What can I do?"

Blue eyes opened, locked on the door to the hallway and beyond. The undiluted sorrow in his gaze tore at Garrick.

He didn't know what the hell was going on in Rhian's head, but he knew that if Rhian got up and left, he'd never come back.

He put a hand on Rhian's back, his touch light. "Will you stay here tonight?"

Rhian rolled over and searched Garrick's face for something. He wished he knew what.

It was a long time before Rhian nodded.

Garrick slowly crawled from the bed, then reached to pull Rhian up.

"Wait."

Garrick froze, his hand suspended above the bed.

Rhian dug in his pocket and drew out a sheet of notebook paper. Without a word, he handed it to Garrick.

Garrick unfolded the note and frowned down at the blackmail demand for a good long time.

Shit.

Refolding the paper, he put it aside and turned a singular focus to the tasks needed to get them both in bed. Rhian allowed Garrick to pull him to his feet and strip him. He never took his watchful gaze off Garrick's face.

Rage burned in Garrick's gut, but he kept his face blank and movements steady. He shucked his clothes and threw them on the floor with Rhian's. God, how he wanted to rip that note into tiny pieces and burn it, all the while cursing its author to the outer reaches of hell. He didn't do or say any of those things. Right now, his only concern was Rhian.

He tugged down the covers and took comfort when Rhian, beautiful and naked and scared witless of something, crawled beneath the sheets.

Garrick slid in behind him, giving him plenty of space. He wanted to wrap himself around his friend and hold on for dear life, but he wrestled back that need and satisfied himself with towing the heavy covers up to their necks as they settled on their sides facing one another.

Rhian's gaze was clear. Sadness still tugged at the corners of his eyes, but not a hint of the panic remained.

"What are you going to do?" Garrick asked quietly.

Rhian sighed. "I don't know." He explained where and when he'd found the note. "I think it might be Steve."

Garrick nodded.

"Maybe I should pay it. At least until this thing with the Bruins is settled, one way or another."

"Can you talk to him?" Garrick asked. He would have preferred to strangle the bastard, but he kept that to himself. Rhian had to decide what to do. Garrick's job was to support that decision.

"I don't know. He's pretty fucked up. This whole thing is fucked up."

There was no arguing with that. "You know he'll never stop asking you for money if you pay."

"I know. But what if he outs you? What if he has proof?"

Garrick cupped Rhian's jaw in his hand and leaned in until they were almost nose to nose. "Do *not* worry about me, do you understand? Whatever decision you make, you make the one that's right for you."

"But the deal? The league?"

"I don't think they'd care, and fuck them if they do. I'll warn Savannah, but that's it as far as protecting me, okay?"

Rhian looked like he wanted to argue, but Garrick held his gaze, narrowing his eyes until Rhian nodded, reluctantly. Garrick released the breath he'd been holding.

"We don't know if there's proof," Rhian said slowly.

Garrick racked his brain for a time they might have been seen or heard and came up blank, unless someone could see into his second-story bedroom window. He fought the urge to jump out of bed and close the curtains. "I don't think there can be."

Rhian nodded. "Yeah. I'm not going to pay."

Garrick ran a thumb along one of Rhian's cheekbones. "Okay."

Rhian's eyes fluttered shut and Garrick traced a pattern on his skin for a while. The warm bed, late hour, and emotionally draining evening dragged them toward sleep. Garrick barely had the wherewithal to roll over and switch off the light. When he turned back, Rhian surprised him with a hand on his chest.

"Garrick?"

"Yeah?"

"I'm sorry you have to trade Justin."

He put a hand over Rhian's. "Me too."

"But I know you're doing the right thing. Anyone who

knows you will understand that."

Garrick swallowed past the lump in his throat. "Thanks."

Rhian pulled his hand from Garrick's and rolled away. Garrick's arms twitched with the need to drag him back. Then his sweet, panicky, confusing-as-all-hell lover scooted across the bed and planted his ass in Garrick's lap, wriggling back until his shoulders were tucked against Garrick's chest.

Garrick spooned around him, holding on way too tight. "Thanks," he whispered again.

Chapter Seventeen

The next evening, Rhian paced the tiny confines of his living room with his phone clutched in his hand. He was trying to get up the courage to call and cancel his dinner plans with Garrick when the phone rang. He nearly dropped it.

Jesus, he was strung a little tight tonight.

Sergio's name popped up on the screen a second before he answered. "What's up?"

"My friend, are you sitting down?"

Quite suddenly, his ass landed on his landlord's brand new coffee table. "Oh my god."

"Well, you can thank god, or you can thank me, but either way you report for duty in Boston in one week."

One week! He started laughing. Hysterically. "Have you told the Ice Cats yet?"

"Dude! You land an NHL contract and that's your first question?"

Rhian laughed again. This was so fucked up. He didn't know what to say. What to do. His dreams were coming true and his first thought was that he only had seven days until he left Garrick. His laughter started to sound a little maniacal, so he choked it back and got the details from Sergio.

The contract was through the end of the season. Then "they would see", but if he didn't stay in Boston and he didn't fuck up, he would get moved to the Bruin's feeder team in Providence. From there, he knew he could work his way back onto the ice at the Boston Garden. For good.

He hung up with Sergio, grabbed his coat, and ran out the door. There was only one person he wanted to share this moment with.

He was tearing onto the highway before he had second thoughts. He and Garrick probably shouldn't be alone together.

Hell, his blackmailer could be watching right now. But that wasn't what worried him. Not really.

The trouble was all the emotions crowding in his head and heart. Twice today alone he'd caught himself watching Garrick like some love-sick puppy. At one point, Rhian was sure Mike had caught him at it, too, but Mike had laughed about something else and moved on. Thank god.

After that, Rhian had decided he couldn't spend any more time alone with Garrick. He'd planned to call Garrick and tell him he wouldn't be over for dinner, hoping that if he ended it now, he could get over whatever the hell was wrong with him and go back to being Garrick's friend. With some time.

Now he only had seven days left. Seven days until he wouldn't see Garrick again until he moved to Boston to be with Savannah. Seven days to do as he wished, then months in Boston with Garrick's girlfriend to remind him why he was going to have to get the fuck over it. Seven days until the mutually agreed-upon return to just friendship.

Seven days to indulge.

A thrill shot down his spine. He knew what he wanted. Physically, at least. Emotionally, he was a big hot mess. But the sex? He was crystal clear on what he wanted there.

God, who knew good news would make him so fucking horny? He laughed as the miles flew by, still buzzed on adrenaline when he parked his car behind Garrick's farmhouse, hiding it from the street. The good feelings carried him right to the back porch before he paused.

He wasn't acting like himself at all.

He'd never had anyone to share this kind of news with, so it was strange and new. And nice. Through the backdoor's window, he watched Garrick move around the kitchen and felt warm, in spite of the winter winds ripping through his coat. He grasped the doorknob, ready to let himself into the house, knowing he was welcome. Expected. He cherished that feeling.

This must be what it feels like to come home.

His hand slipped from the knob.

Garrick was busy painting a thick maple ginger glaze, judging by the jars scattered across the granite island, over what appeared to be salmon. At his elbow, a pile of fresh cut broccoli waited to be tossed into the steaming pot on the stove. Two wine glasses and an open bottle sat on the kitchen table alongside two places set with cloth napkins and heavy stoneware plates that suited the room, and the man, perfectly.

It was all so...*domestic*. Foreign.

Garrick turned around and the ache in Rhian's chest was replaced by an unwilling snort of humor. Garrick's bright red apron read: *Give Blood. Play Hockey.*

Garrick looked up and the smile in his eyes pulled Rhian through the door.

"Seriously, Garrick, where did you get that apron?"

Garrick glanced down at his chest, which dwarfed what was probably a normal-size apron. "You like it?"

"I love it."

Garrick grinned. Rhian's heart skipped a beat.

"Maybe I'll let you take it with you to Boston," Garrick said. He chucked the marinade brush onto the counter and reached for Rhian.

Rhian let rip a victorious whoop as Garrick yanked him into a hug. Their chests crashed together, then Rhian was holding on for dear life as his feet left the ground, laughter bouncing off the walls as the last of his disbelief, the final traces of shock, were swept away by unadulterated joy.

He'd done it. He'd made it to the NHL. The brass fucking ring.

His feet hit the ground with a thud and he stepped out of his first-ever bear hug with a light heart and bone-deep gratitude. That was just what he'd needed. To tell someone who understood. Who cared. For the first time in his life, there was someone in the world who gave a crap. About him. His dreams, his hard work, his achievements.

He would never be able to explain this to anyone, let alone

Garrick, but he couldn't let it pass without acknowledging it to himself. This was good. And he was happy.

So was Garrick, judging by his huge smile and shining eyes. He grabbed Rhian's face between his hands and planted a loud kiss on his forehead. Rhian laughed. It was the damndest thing. He'd seen countless fathers do the same to their sons at hockey practice over the years. No one had ever done it to him, though.

Garrick left him grinning like a simpleton and bent to check the racks in the oven, his faded jeans tight across his gorgeous butt. Rhian's jeans got a lot tighter too.

Happiness really did make him horny.

Searching for a distraction, he poured them both a glass of wine then propped a hip against the counter and watched Garrick. He tried to focus on his lover's confidence and competence in the kitchen— not his broad shoulders and thick thighs.

For a guy with a terrible reputation as a ladies' man off the ice and a hard-ass on it, Garrick was frighteningly comfortable flipping through his Martha Stewart cookbook. Rhian bit his lip to keep from laughing.

He managed to contain himself until Garrick pulled out a huge chipped mixing bowl and set it on the counter next to a giant block of butter before gathering various baking supplies from the cabinets. When, after digging around on one particular shelf, Garrick triumphantly brandished a bag of chocolate chips, Rhian broke.

An uncontrollable guffaw burst from him, his laughter only getting worse when Garrick slowly put the chocolate down on the counter and looked at him with one brow raised.

"What's so funny?"

He heard the warning in Garrick's tone and grabbed his wine glass. After almost snarfing its contents up his nose with another chuckle, he put it back down.

That one eyebrow arched higher.

"Nothing," he blurted. "Really. It's just, well…you're making chocolate chip cookies, aren't you? You're actually making me chocolate chip cookies. From scratch."

"Yeah, so?"

"It's just so…so…"

"What?"Garrick challenged, his gaze narrowing.

"Well…"

Garrick stared. Waiting.

"Cute."

Garrick chuckled. It had been a long time since anyone had called him cute, but he didn't mind. He didn't even mind being laughed at. He was, after all, standing in his kitchen in a silly apron, making his boyfriend chocolate chip cookies.

His boyfriend? Ack! Not boyfriend, of course. Lover. Whatever.

He put that thought away for another time. Right now he was having too much fun enjoying Rhian's light mood and easy laughter. In the year he'd known Rhian, he'd never seen him so relaxed. So perfectly *happy.*

He could only imagine how great it felt. He'd been riding on a high since he'd gotten the call from Rupert, telling him the Bruins had made their move. He'd checked the clock a thousand times, waiting for Rhian to get here, worried he would cancel. He'd had to exert a truck-load of restraint to resist storming out to his back porch and dragging the man into the house when he'd hesitated to come in.

But somehow Rhian had made it through the door and Garrick could see right away something was different. He supposed being drafted into the NHL would change any man, but it was more than that. The tension that had buzzed beneath the surface since that night in Charlottetown was gone. Rhian was here, with him, fully.

His friend was back, only now he was openly staring at Garrick's ass when he bent to retrieve something from the cabinets. He contemplated turning around and letting Rhian get an eyeful of what his attention was doing to the fit of Garrick's jeans.

No. Dinner, then cookies, then *bed, you damn horn-dog.* He had a plan and he was sticking to it.

Standing at his shoulder, Rhian peered down at what Garrick was doing, a wide grin on his face. Garrick chuckled again. Who knew the guy would be so excited about fresh-baked cookies?

Garrick carefully measured out the ingredients, nearly dumping the cup of sugar on the counter when Rhian's lips brushed the back of his neck.

Holy hell.

Rhian didn't let up. Garrick kept working, determined to finish the damn cookie dough while Rhian drove him out of his ever-loving mind with a zillion little nibbles and licks along each vertebrae from his nape to the collar of his shirt. Garrick did a goddamn admirable job of keeping it together until Rhian's hips snugged up against his ass. A big hand spread across his stomach to hold him in place while his errant and intensely distracting lover nudged his stiff cock between his ass cheeks.

Garrick promptly forgot the recipe he'd known by heart since he was twelve.

Fuck the plan.

Rhian's eyes went wide when Garrick spun them and shoved Rhian's ass back against the counter, their hips close but not quite touching. Pink splotches rode high on Rhian's cheekbones, his eyes dilated, and Garrick smiled. He dipped his head and brushed his nose against Rhian's.

"Are you done having fun?"

Rhian looked right at him. "No."

There was no mistaking the challenge in Rhian's eyes. Garrick's cock launched into a pitched wrestling match with his fly.

He pressed Rhian's hands flat on the countertop and held

them there, warm under his palms as he eased closer. His voice was little more than a rumble when he whispered in Rhian's ear. "Naughty."

It was a promise, not an admonishment.

Rhian's flushed deepened, his eyes heavy, and that low sound—the perfect combination of a moan and a whimper—caught in his throat.

Garrick bit back a groan.

Despite his brazenness moments before, Rhian gave himself over, ceding control. Never in his life had Garrick guessed how fucking hot that would be. But then, this would never interest him with anyone else. Had never even crossed his mind. But Rhian was his physical equal. Hell, probably his better. This only worked because Rhian willingly surrendered control while they both knew he could take it back at any time.

It was hotter than hell.

Rhian stood passively and waited for Garrick to do as he pleased, trusting him to please them both. He gasped when Garrick rubbed their lips together, then dragged his mouth over Rhian's cheek, his jaw, nibbling as he went. Rhian's head tipped back to give him room.

"You taste good," Garrick murmured, licking a slow line up the corded muscles of Rhian's neck.

"So do you."

Garrick caught Rhian as he attempted to slither to his knees at Garrick's feet.

Temptation tore at him. "No." He held onto Rhian with two hands, and his willpower by a string. "I have plans for you and I don't want to do anything that might—" He stopped, sucked in a breath, and crushed his aching erection against Rhian's belly. "I won't risk ruining your voice. I want to hear you shout my name when you come with me inside you."

Rhian inhaled sharply and goosebumps popped along the strong column of his neck. His hips rocked forward and Garrick almost staggered back from the force of his need. Anticipation had Garrick cranked so tight, he wanted to throw back his head and howl from it. He fought not to rush, to drag Rhian down on the floor in his kitchen and do everything and anything right then.

He wouldn't. It felt urgent. Necessary, even. But that didn't mean he wouldn't take his sweet-ass time getting Rhian ready. Or maybe that was Rhian's sweet-ass time?

Rhian bucked again, forcing Garrick to grasp the edge of the counter to meet his thrust. His thigh slid between Rhian's, pressing home. Rhian moaned and rocked again, jamming his cock against Garrick's quad.

The friction was sweet. Unstoppable. They were humping each other, fully clothed, like a couple of teenagers, but it didn't matter. He captured Rhian's mouth and shuddered when Rhian returned his kiss with fervent licks and desperate sounds. Hips tilted, legs shifted, their bodies searching for the right angle and pressure.

Garrick clutched at the counter and gasped when his fingers sank into the block of butter.

Inspiration struck.

He grappled one-handed with the button of Rhian's jeans, struggling to wrench the clasp open. Rhian groaned into his mouth.

Garrick tore their lips apart, panting. "Help me."

Only then did Rhian move his hands from the countertop where Garrick had planted them. A bolt of awareness almost leveled Garrick.

Rhian's hands shook as he unbuttoned his jeans and eased the zipper past his straining erection. The moment his fly was down, he shoved his jeans to his thighs and his cock sprang free.

In spite of the rush of blood in his ears and the thud of need in his balls, Garrick was lucid enough to wonder if the no-underwear thing would ever get less hot.

Nope.

He touched his forehead to Rhian's and stared down at the fierce plum-shaped crown pressed between their bellies. God, he was going to miss this, miss Rhian.

The idea made him a little frantic.

He nudged his hips forward. Rhian understood. He shoved Garrick's shirt and apron high on his chest, worked open his button fly with few rough jerks, and shoved Garrick's jeans and briefs down to his knees.

Garrick growled, his head spinning when hot skin pressed against his, their cocks aligned from stem to tip. The grind of their hips and the heaving of their chests created a delicious, if awkward, friction.

He had just the thing to ease their way.

Dragging his hand from the counter, he slipped it between their bodies and wrapped his fingers around both of their cocks. He slicked up to the heads, rubbing the smooth cream into silky skin.

Rhian gasped. "Jesus, Garrick. What is that?"

He smiled. "Butter."

Rhian's mouth dropped open as Garrick ran his slippery fingers down the length of their shafts. Rhian actually gurgled. Garrick laughed while he dredged the fingers of his other hand through the butter.

Forming a slick tunnel with both his hands, Garrick set a furious pace, leaping into overdrive to match the knock of his heart and the stutter of Rhian's hips. His eyes wanted to roll back into his head, but he held on. He refused to relinquish the pleasure of watching Rhian's face.

No hesitation. No fear. No questions. Just ecstasy. Fierce concentration A little smile hovering on his lips. He'd returned his hands to the countertop, palms flat, fingers wide where Garrick had put them.

"Keep them there," Garrick growled.

Rhian's eyes flashed up to meet his and he groaned, long and low. His cock swelled further. Garrick pumped his hands faster. The heat building between them melted the butter, turning it to a slick, clinging liquid that slid down their shafts. He smoothed one hand lower, skimming his fingers over their balls and along Rhian's perineum.

"God," Rhian gasped. "That's so..."

"Obscene?"

"Yes," he hissed. It didn't sound like a bad thing.

Garrick pressed his finger harder, higher, and Rhian lifted onto his toes. With every downward stroke along their shafts, some sound tore from Rhian. A plea. A moan. Affirmations. Garrick's name.

The sweet music filled Garrick's ears and he drove them faster, his heart expanding as every other muscle in his body constricted, preparing for the climax that hovered just out of reach. His gaze met Rhian's wide and impossibly blue eyes.

Rhian's cock swelled. The heat of his climax filled Garrick's hand before it registered on Rhian's face.

Powerful. Beautiful.

As if Rhian had let go of the counter and grabbed Garrick with two hands, he yanked Garrick right over the edge with him.

Chapter Eighteen

Rhian took a bite from a cookie and smiled at Garrick. "I have to admit, the warm cookie thing is great."

"Damn right it is," Garrick grumbled.

Rhian smiled, not worried that Garrick was truly hurt that Rhian had teased him earlier.

They'd sat down to dinner an hour ago, having discarded their shirts and Garrick's apron after their adventure with the butter. Neither had been in any hurry to dispel the lax-muscled euphoria brought on by mind-scrambling orgasms.

Rhian still wasn't. He took his time, admiring Garrick's bare chest. Again.

The damn man had only done up three buttons on his jeans. Rhian savored the low hum of arousal that had buzzed beneath his skin throughout their meal. What wasn't to like about his unfettered view of Garrick's wide pecs, cinnamon brown nipples, and the tight twist of his belly button?

If the warmth in Garrick's eyes was any indication, the appreciation was mutual. Rhian shifted in his chair, shamelessly flexing his abs.

Garrick leaped from his seat and popped his last cookie into his mouth. He insisted he didn't need help as he made efficient work of clearing the table. Rhian lingered over what remained of his dessert and watched Garrick move around the kitchen.

The moment Rhian took his final bite of cookie, his plate was whisked away and deposited in the dishwasher.

"You in a hurry?" Rhian asked with a slow smile.

Garrick tugged him up out of his chair.

Rhian's heart rate doubled.

Rather than answer the question, Garrick kissed him thoroughly. Or maybe that *was* the answer.

The kiss was slow, their tongues easing from one mouth to the other. Their heads angled and re-angled to change the depth and direction of the kiss. Garrick's hands slid to Rhian's ass and pulled him close.

Rhian could stand there and make out with Garrick all night. This was another in the long list of new experiences he was racking up. All his previous lovers had gone into it with the goal of finding release—the same goal he'd had. These long, lingering kisses weren't about that, and he enjoyed the hell out of it. For now, for however long they stood here, this was enough.

They came up for air with a gasp. Rhian shivered when Garrick's long fingers traced over his face.

"What do you want to do?" Garrick asked, his voice rough.

The steel bar in Rhian's pants, poking at Garrick's hip, should have made the answer pretty obvious.

Garrick chuckled, but his expression was serious. "We could snuggle on the couch and watch TV, if you want. Or sit here longer." Garrick swallowed. "Or go up to bed. Whatever you want."

Rhian thought it was sweet that Garrick gave him options. Was letting him decide. But seriously, who was he kidding?

Rhian peeled Garrick's hand off his ass and threaded their fingers together. Garrick might like to be in charge most of the time—and god fucking knew that was really working for Rhian—but now his big, fierce lover followed him, docile, as Rhian towed him through the dining room and up the stairs.

They made it as far as the upstairs hallway before Garrick's true nature reasserted itself. He pulled Rhian in for a long, stirring kiss, his hand wrapped around the back of Rhian's head. *Better.* Rhian happily ceded control, smiling when Garrick's lips left his to skim over his cheek and under his chin. Garrick's tongue tickled. Teeth nipped. Rhian shamelessly bent his head in whatever direction necessary to grant Garrick access wherever he wanted. Rhian tucked his chin to his chest and shuddered at the sting of Garrick's bite on the back of his neck.

Their bodies brushed, skin rubbing over skin, as Garrick moved to stand behind him, his lips never ceasing their gentle torture. Rhian hummed low in his throat, uncaring what Garrick did next. It all felt so damn good.

Garrick slid warm hands around Rhian's flanks to his belly and pulled him back against a wall of heat and muscle. His knees shook as Garrick walked them forward, toward the bedroom and whatever would come next. The broad flat of Garrick's tongue skidded over his shoulder and his teeth took hold. Rhian gasped and stumbled.

His shoulder caught on the doorjamb and brought them up short, plastering Garrick to his back in the process. Garrick stopped torturing him and wrapped his long arms around Rhian's waist to steady them both.

Rhian stared at the huge bed as if he'd never seen it before.

This is it.

Nerves sprang to life in his belly, but it didn't change what he wanted.

Garrick pressed his lips to Rhian's ear. "We won't do anything you don't want to do."

That was nice, but it wasn't the issue. He shook his head, grabbing Garrick's arms when he moved back.

"No, please. Hold on."

He'd intended only to stop Garrick's retreat, but Garrick took his words literally and held him tighter. It wasn't as good as when Garrick lay down on top of him, but it was close. Rhian closed his eyes and relaxed.

"Is something wrong?" Garrick asked quietly.

"Nothing. God, nothing at all. I just thought I should mention...umm...I've never... I mean, I've done it. It's just that I..." He tried to find the right word and came up blank. "I was, you know, the one giving. I've never..."

"Bottomed?" Garrick supplied softly.

Rhian squirmed, his ass clenching. "Yeah."

"You don't have to—"

"I want to." As if it weren't obvious by the way his ass was writhing against Garrick's cock. "I just thought you should know."

Garrick's warm lips brushed his neck again. Rhian didn't know what to expect in response to his awkward admission. Certainly not Garrick's rough voice sighing in his ear.

"Thank you."

Rhian made that sound again. The one he only made for Garrick. He wanted to pretend it was a manly grunt but he knew it for what it was. The man made him whimper.

Thank you?

Garrick was really, really welcome.

Garrick held Rhian tighter and closed his eyes. He'd guessed Rhian didn't have a lot of experience, but he hadn't imagined he would be given this gift.

Garrick was determined not to fuck it up.

First, he had to regain command over his legs, in particular his knees, which had turned to jelly when Rhian more or less offered Garrick his virgin ass.

With a lurch, he stepped around Rhian and into the room, drawing Rhian toward the bed. Rhian was a little wide-eyed, his movements stiff. When Garrick stopped, they collided.

He rubbed his cheek along Rhian's. "Relax."

Rhian's jerky nod confirmed that telling him to do it wasn't going to work. Hardly a surprise. Garrick ran his hands over Rhian's bare chest, trying to soothe him. The hard lines of Rhian's belly jumped beneath his fingertips, his breath unsteady as Garrick traced the swells and valleys of his abs.

When he eased his hands into the waist of Rhian's jeans, his lover stopped breathing all together. Garrick began to worry Rhian would freak out again, but when he slid his hand down to protect Rhian's junk from his zipper, he found him hard as stone.

Nervous, yes. But still right on board.

Garrick stripped them both in a matter of seconds. He caught Rhian staring at his dick, licking his lips. Garrick smiled and claimed that talented mouth in a ravenous kiss.

Rhian surged against him, his cock running along the groove that joined Garrick's hip to his groin. Garrick moaned, gripping Rhian's ass to bring him to where he wanted him.

He fell to the bed, holding Rhian close, rolling above him when they bounced on the mattress. Rhian threaded his fingers into Garrick's hair and thrust his tongue into every corner of Garrick's mouth. Garrick's heart galloped, his body flushed and hot all over as his nervous lover devoured him.

Sweat broke out across his brow. God, now *he* was nervous. He wanted so badly for this to be good for Rhian. Perfect.

Rhian ran his fingers over Garrick's head, nails dragging against his scalp, and moaned. He spread his legs and lifted his knees to settle Garrick into the cradle of his thighs, their erections pressed close and hot between them.

"Jesus," Garrick muttered when he finally tore his mouth loose.

A ghost of a smile flashed across Rhian's face, his only response a long slow thrust of his hips against Garrick's.

"Jesus."

He'd been worried Rhian would cancel tonight, but he'd shown up. He'd been prepared to convince Rhian it was okay for them to be intimate again, but Rhian had pulled him to his bedroom without hesitation. And he'd been absolutely certain it would take all his patience and talent to convince Rhian to let him fuck him, and despite his apparent nerves, the damn man had *asked for it.*

Rhian grabbed Garrick's ass and ground their bodies together.

God was he asking for it.

Garrick kissed him again, his groan stopping with an

abrupt grunt when Rhian skated the pad on his finger over Garrick's tightly clenched anus.

"You like?" Rhian asked with a devilish smile.

It was totally obvious he liked. Liked a lot.

The tip of Rhian's finger wedged into the tight ring of muscle and wriggled. He didn't have to grind Garrick down on top of him anymore. Garrick's hips danced, their cocks rolling and sliding between their bellies.

He screwed his eyes shut and told himself to pull it together. Groping for the bedside table, he managed to retrieve the lube and condoms without dumping the entire contents onto the floor. He tossed the supplies on the bed and waited to see Rhian's reaction.

Rhian picked up the bottle of lube and read the label like he was browsing the aisle of the goddamn grocery store. Garrick chuckled, and Rhian's eyes cut to him, narrowing.

Rhian's slow smile should have been warning enough, but Garrick still twitched with surprise when Rhian popped the cap open and poured a stream of the slippery liquid down Garrick's ass. Rhian's fingers captured the drips and rubbed them into Garrick's skin, circling the tight knot of muscles with two fingers before pressing against Garrick's perineum.

Garrick slammed his eyes shut and groaned. Shit, that felt amazing.

"You love this," Rhian said with a hint of awe.

Garrick nodded rapidly and arched his back to shove his ass into Rhian's hands.

"So you don't just—"

"*Fuck.*" Garrick barked the word in response to what Rhian was doing to him, not to play fill-in-the-blank.

"Would you let me fuck you?" Rhian asked with nothing short of wonder in his voice.

"Yes." Without a doubt.

"Oh." Rhian bit his lower lip and Garrick snapped out of his euphoria long enough to make himself clear.

He locked gazes with Rhian. "Not tonight."

The sweetest little smile, almost a smirk, curled Rhian's lips. "No?"

Garrick fell into those deep blue eyes, entranced by the spark of humor, the glow of happiness there. What on earth had he ever done to deserve this man?

Garrick ran his hands down Rhian's sides and slid them beneath his ass. His finger teased over Rhian's hole. The muscles fluttered against his touch, responding instantly without clenching.

"Mine," he growled.

Rhian nodded and blood throbbed in Garrick's cock, swelling it further. Capturing Rhian's mouth, he distracted them both with long, drugging kisses. He hadn't meant to sound so possessive, like he was staking a claim for more than this one night. They only had until Rhian left for Boston.

The thought made Garrick's pounding heart ache. *Damn it.*

He danced his tongue along Rhian's and focused on just that. The connection. *Now.* His assault on Rhian's mouth ended with an abrupt grunt when Rhian breached his ass with a finger and sank it in to the second knuckle.

He shoved back against that delicious pressure and helped Rhian go deeper. His body clenched around the invasion.

Garrick held Rhian's face in both hands and kissed him harder, deeper, trying to communicate what he couldn't even figure out himself. What he was feeling.

Rhian's hand slowed and Garrick almost believed he'd captured Rhian's undivided attention with his lips when Rhian tucked a second finger in next to the first.

"Yes!" Garrick hissed, rocking back to embed the digits more firmly.

Rhian laughed, actually *laughed*. He shoved his fingers deeper and started a steady pump into Garrick's ass. "God, look at you."

Garrick thought he should be offended, but he couldn't be

bothered. Rhian's eyes danced, his smile wide. He spread his fingers, stretching Garrick open, searching Garrick's face for his every reaction. Garrick didn't hold back, groaning over the pleasure Rhian teased from his body.

"You're going to have to stop that or this is going to be over before it starts."

Rhian froze. Garrick chuckled.

Good to know their priorities were still aligned.

With a sigh of regret, he pulled away and forced Rhian's fingers to slip from his tender hole. He clenched against the emptiness left behind and considered retrieving a butt plug and begging Rhian to shove it in him.

Then he knelt between Rhian's thighs, looked down at the man sprawled across the bed beneath him, and knew he didn't need anything else.

Savannah had thought Rhian was gorgeous before? Garrick didn't know how he'd find words to describe him as he was now. It would be a gift, to be able to share something as beautiful as this with her.

The warmth in Rhian's gaze tugged at Garrick. His smile hypnotic.

Garrick smiled back, slowly, flooded with gratitude for Savannah. For her generosity. For her love.

For Rhian.

Chapter Nineteen

Rhian lay on the bed and stared up at Garrick as a slow smile spread across his face. Goddamn, Garrick was gorgeous like this. Flushed, breathing hard, without a stitch of clothing so Rhian could enjoy every inch of his wide shoulders, deep chest, and tapered hips.

He trailed his gaze over the curve of Garrick's ass as he reached to retrieve the lube. Rhian shuddered, imagining what it would be like to sink into those depths, to wrap his hands around those hips and feel those firm cheeks against his belly.

He wanted that. But not as much as he wanted to feel Garrick in him. Tonight. It was shocking, since the idea had never had much appeal before now. But with Garrick it was different.

Rhian stifled a chuckle. How many times had he said that in the last year?

It was always different with Garrick.

He rubbed his hand over the hollow ache in his chest. The ache that had been his companion for a while now. Far longer than they'd been lovers, if he were honest with himself.

He shunted aside the fear before Garrick could see it and bring their adventure to a halt. Rhian had no doubt he would, and it wasn't like Rhian could explain. He didn't understand it himself. What mattered now was *this*. They had one week, then—Rhian swore to himself—he'd get over it.

No problem.

Garrick touched his face. "If I asked what you're thinking right now, would you tell me?"

Rhian smiled, shoving the sadness in a little box, right next to the fear. "Nope."

"Will you ever tell me?"

Rhian looked to the ceiling, pretending to give it some

thought, before he grinned at Garrick. "Nope."

Garrick growled good-naturedly and ran his hands down Rhian's sensitive ribs. His overwhelmed nervous system didn't process the tickling fingers as anything but more sensual pleasure until Garrick dug into his armpits.

Laughter burst from him and he squirmed, trying to escape.

"Stop! Stop!" he gasped, howling as he rolled away.

Garrick wasn't having it. He stopped Rhian's desperate attempt to reach the side of the bed and dragged him back to the middle of the mattress. Rhian was still wheezing when Garrick spun him onto his stomach and lay down on top of him.

Rhian went utterly lax. Garrick chuckled and drew his arms from his sides to fold them above his head, nibbling along the back of his neck as he arranged Rhian however he wished.

Rhian closed his eyes and hummed. He'd never known he had so many damn hot spots back there. But then, he'd never known the power, the *peace* that was to be found pinned under this man.

Garrick took his time exploring with lips and teeth. Rhian lay there in heaven. He murmured a protest when Garrick lifted himself away and knelt between his wide-spread thighs.

"Ready?" Garrick asked.

Shivers ran down Rhian's spine.

He answered by drawing his knees up beneath him and lifting his ass into the air, his face smashed to the mattress. It was shameless, but then there was no shame to be found anywhere in Rhian. He was ready. He wanted this.

Garrick groaned and wrapped his big hands around the backs of Rhian's thighs before sliding them up to his ass to pull the globes apart. Rhian could imagine the portrait he must make, and he smiled against the cool sheets beneath his hot cheek. His mind buzzed with a tranquil static that blocked out the rest of the world. There was only Garrick, him, this bed, and now.

The cool touch of Garrick's finger plucked him from his quiet daze. He'd been so far into his own head, he hadn't noticed Garrick reaching for the lube. He dragged his eyes open and saw the empty condom packet. His ass clenched.

Garrick's quiet murmur soothed and his thick finger slipped into Rhian's ass without resistance. It felt incredible. The muscle gave easily, the sensitive nerves lining his entrance quivering as he felt the rub of skin, the folds of Garrick's knuckles. Rhian swore he could feel each hair on that finger as it pushed deep, not stopping until Garrick's hand came to rest against the crease of his ass.

Yes. Good.

Even better was the slow, steady pump as Garrick worked his finger in and out. It was hypnotic. A second finger slid in and Rhian mumbled something that sounded a lot like, "perfect."

On the next withdrawal, Garrick spread his fingers. Rhian moaned and arched his back as the thrill of the burn rippled over him.

He wanted more.

His wish was granted with another press. Another retreat. Rhian shifted his hips, rolling them back to meet the force of Garrick's thrust, twitching them forward to maximize the stretch.

Garrick ran a wide palm up his spine, warming his skin, layering another sensation on top of all the others.

He hardly noticed the tip of the third finger slipping between the two scissoring him open. His muscles yielded, willingly. Then Garrick thrust deep and the stretch was huge.

Rhian's mouth fell open in a silent gasp, the air locked in his lungs.

Garrick didn't draw back, his fingers shoved as far as they could go, the ring of muscles clamped around them like a vise. His other hand continued to trail up and down Rhian's back, the heel of his palm digging until the tension bled away.

Rhian's shoulders sank into the mattress, his face buried in the sheets. Garrick bumped his hand forward, forcing that damn sound up out of Rhian's chest, over and over.

Nothing had ever felt so good. So completely freeing.

When at last Garrick withdrew his hand, Rhian moaned at the loss. The brush of plastic and cool lube cut the sound off with a gasp.

Garrick's belly bumped Rhian's ass and the thick stalk of his erection jammed against the burning muscles of Rhian's anus. He bent over and pressed a kiss between Rhian's shoulder blades.

"Yes?" Garrick's lips barely brushed his ear.

"Yes."

"Grab onto the headboard."

Rhian snapped his eyes open. Garrick's weight lifted from his back and he reached for the wooden support while Garrick's big hands wrapped around his hips.

Oh hell, *yes.*

Garrick stared down at the long, muscled back stretched out before him and swallowed hard. That so much power and strength was like putty in his hands was somehow miraculous and insanely hot.

Shifting his fingers for a better grip on Rhian's hip, he lined up the head of his cock and eased forward.

Tight muscles resisted in spite of his preparation. A ripple of tension flowed over Rhian's back and ass. Garrick didn't retreat, keeping the pressure steady and strong. The head of his cock flattened against so much resistance until, with a gasp from Rhian, Garrick slipped inside.

"Oh God, Garrick. That's fucking amazing."

Yes. It. Is.

Garrick stared down at his cock locked in Rhian's body and held still to let Rhian's muscles adjust. Relax. Also, he needed a second to get his shit together.

Rhian either didn't understand how close Garrick was to losing it, or he just didn't care. He used his powerful arms, biceps bulging, to shove himself back. Hard.

Garrick met his strength, clutching the hot, sweat-slicked skin of Rhian's hips, and sank his cock into Rhian's ass with one long push.

Holy shit, it was too much. As soon as his belly came to rest against Rhian's firm, round butt, he fell forward, wrapped his arms around the long arch of Rhian's torso, and buried his face in soft blond curls.

"Rhian."

Rhian nodded, as if he understood.

God, he doesn't know the half of it yet.

Garrick rotated his hips and Rhian gasped, his head thrown back so their faces were side by side.

Garrick did it again.

And again.

His cock throbbed against Rhian's tight walls, the ring of muscles clamping down around the base of Garrick's shaft rippling in reaction to the shifting pressure.

Garrick was lost. Lost to the cry of his name from Rhian's lips. To the firestorm growing in his balls. The electricity singing along his spine.

Rhian's lips brushed his cheek and he met the awkward kiss fervently. The angle was rough, necks straining, legs shaking, and Rhian alone was supporting all their weight. It was messy and hot and not enough.

Their mouths slid apart. "This isn't working," Garrick muttered.

"What?" Rhian cried, his hips bucking back and forcing Garrick's cock deeper. Rhian made that damn whimper.

Garrick huffed out a strangled laugh and hauled himself upright. With a long, slow glide, he pulled his cock from Rhian's welcoming body.

"No," Rhian groaned, looking back at Garrick in confusion.

Garrick didn't bother to explain. He grabbed Rhian's leg and heaved, flipping him onto his back. He stared up at Garrick wide-eyed as Garrick pulled up his thighs until he was bent in half, his knees pressed to his chest.

With a sharp jab, Garrick punched past Rhian's fluttering sphincter and slammed home.

Rhian rocked his ass up to bring Garrick even deeper. *"Garrick!"*

The sound of his name bouncing off the wall, the look on Rhian's face, stole the last of Garrick's control. He'd planned to go slow. To ease Rhian into this. Instead, his hips snapped in demanding thrusts and worked his cock into the heat and clench of Rhian's body. He fucked Rhian hard, with long, deep, shattering strokes, pulling back until only the head remained locked in Rhian's ass, then plunging deep, until their bodies met with a dull thump.

Rhian undulated beneath him, muscles bunching and releasing, meeting his powerful drives with equal strength.

It was too good. There was so little time left.

Garrick captured Rhian's mouth in a deep kiss. Rhian's tongue tangled with his and he wrapped his powerful legs around Garrick's ribs.

Garrick pulled him closer, chests pressed tight. He ran a hand over Rhian's head and grasped the thick blond curls in his fist to control the depth and angle of the kiss.

Rhian groaned, the sound pure agony and desire. His rigid cock was trapped between their bellies, slipping across their sweat-slicked skin with every thrust.

At this angle and depth, Garrick could do no more than sharp, short thrusts, but it was good. Better than good. It was fucking amazing. He needed to see Rhian's face. Hear his cries and see his mouth fall open when he nailed all the right spots.

He needed to hold him like this. To know it was his face

Rhian saw when he came unglued.

He thrust harder, faster, shifting until Rhian was howling every time Garrick sawed over his prostate. Strong fingers scrabbled at his back.

"Oh fuck!" Rhian cried. "Oh fuck, fuckfuckfuckfuckfuck!" Rhian threw back his head. "*Garrick*!"

The long arc of Rhian's body lifting them both as he wailed Garrick's name to the ceiling, spurts of hot, sticky come firing across their chests. The already unbearably tight ring of muscle around Garrick's shaft clamped down harder, pulling him in deep.

Lightning stroked up Garrick's spine. He pressed his open mouth to the pounding pulse in Rhian's neck, muffling his hoarse cry as his climax exploded out of him. He shook from the force of it, each ripple tearing another sound from his chest, another twitch from his hips.

It went on forever, but it was still too soon when Garrick eased his trembling arms from their death grip around Rhian and pried his fingers from Rhian's curls. Garrick's hands shook as he brushed the tangle of hair from Rhian's forehead.

Dark blue eyes stared up at him, stunned, while Garrick tried to think of what to say.

There were no words.

Chapter Twenty

Rhian swung around the net and watched the puck skim down the ice to Garrick. He told himself to keep his eye on the play, goddamn it, but it was impossible to ignore the way Garrick's long legs pumped as he propelled himself across the ice.

When the puck almost sailed right past Rhian, he thanked god no one from the Bruins was watching and this was only practice. His head was seriously not in the game.

Another first to add to the list.

He'd spent the last three nights curled up in Garrick's bed, in Garrick's arms, where he wanted to be in spite of his certainty that he was only making it worse for himself. He'd thought seven days would be plenty of time to work Garrick out of his system, but Rhian could no longer kid himself. He was masochistically collecting as many memories as possible before he walked away and never looked back.

He didn't have a choice, but it was also the right thing to do. Garrick had Savannah, not to mention a hockey team to run. Rhian had the Bruins, who had paid for his undivided attention. From there, who knew? It didn't matter where, the point was *what*. Hockey. The NHL. Financial security and the achievement of all his dreams.

That the thought of that future left an empty ache in his chest was the clearest and most bitter evidence yet that he should never have chased Garrick back to his hotel room that night. Let alone done any of the things they'd done since.

So why don't I regret a minute of it?

With a sigh, he threw himself back into practice. When they took a break to switch drills, Garrick skated up to him and Mike.

"You guys up for beers tonight?"

Rhian felt a pang of disappointment that Garrick wasn't planning to go straight back to his house and ripping Rhian's clothes off. He startled when Garrick clapped a gloved hand on his shoulder.

"Uh, sure," Rhian said.

"We haven't celebrated your big news," Garrick said.

Rhian stared down at his skate and bit his lip hard, desperately trying not to laugh. They'd celebrated for the past three days, as he was achingly aware every time he sat down.

"Great idea," Mike agreed as the rest of their circle of friends floated over.

"What's up?" Alexei asked.

"Drinks tonight at Quigley's to celebrate Rhian's big move," Garrick announced. "All of us, and if it's all right with Rhian, I thought we could invite the new guy."

Tim cocked his head. "What new guy?"

Rhian had no idea either. They hadn't added anyone to the team in a while, and Justin's replacement wouldn't arrive until next week.

Garrick chuckled. "Rupert!"

Rhian swallowed back a laugh at the expressions, varying from stunned to dismayed, on the guys' faces. Rupert had only been with the team for a week, but he'd already made something of an impression.

"Uh...okay," Alexei said. "Maybe we don't invite all team then, huh?"

Garrick smiled, not entirely disguising his relief, and Rhian felt guilty for almost having laughed.

Garrick needed Rupert to settle in, fast. The fact that Rupert was failing to keep his anxiety at bay, let alone hidden from the team, was a big issue. Worse still, Rupert—the manager of a *professional hockey team*—seemed most nervous when he was around the players. It was a total cluster fuck in the making.

Would Rupert chill out once he got to know some of the

other guys? Rhian could guess that was Garrick's hope.

"Yeah, let's keep it to just us for now," Rhian said.

"Sure," Dave said. "And we've got Justin's going-away thing tomorrow night anyway, right?"

Garrick's smile faltered. Tomorrow night was going to be hell for him, if he even decided to go. He kept telling Rhian it might be better if he made some excuse, since eventually they would all learn he'd had something to do with the trade.

Rhian didn't get why Garrick wouldn't believe his friends would stand by him.

When everyone else skated away, Rhian held Garrick back and addressed the more immediate issue. "You sure about bringing Rupert out with Alexei? If Alexei gets it in his head to pull one of his pranks, I'm not sure Rupert won't end up with PTSD."

Garrick grimaced. "God help me."

Rhian laughed. "I'm kidding. It'll be fine. Put Rupert next to me. We know each other's secrets. Maybe that will make him feel better."

"As long as I get to sit on the other side of you," Garrick murmured, dark promise in his voice.

Rhian's mouth fell open. He quickly looked around to be sure no one else could hear them. They were standing in the middle of the ice, for Christ's sake, and Garrick knew perfectly well how sound traveled out here.

He was about to shoot Garrick the mother of all *completely silent* dirty looks when he caught sight of a lone man sitting in the stands.

"Shit."

Garrick started to turn. "What?"

Rhian grabbed his sleeve. "Don't."

Garrick took a deep breath and dropped his shoulders. "Did someone hear me?" he whispered.

"What?" Rhian had already forgotten about Garrick's

momentary indiscretion a moment before. "No, not that. Steve is sitting over there. Tenth row, over the bench." *Easy shouting distance to all our teammates and the coaching staff.*

Garrick, who had played in this arena for twelve years, didn't bother to look. "Shit."

Rhian forced a bright smile. "That's what I'm saying."

"Should we ask him to leave?"

Rhian shook his head. "I think we should ignore him."

That was what Rhian had been doing for the better part of a week. The time and date for the blackmail drop off had long since come and gone, and he'd continued going about his business as if he'd never seen the note. Maybe Steve thought the wind had ripped it off his windshield?

He looked up at Steve, who stared back, long and hard, before slowly shaking his head back and forth.

Yeah, so much for that.

Garrick stood in the bar at Quigley's and stared slack-jawed at the men walking through the door. He'd stopped by Rupert's office to invite him out with the guys that night, and he'd seemed genuinely pleased to accept. Now Rupert stood in the entryway, pink cheeked from the bitter wind blowing outside, and smiled at Reese like an attendant might smile at one of the inmates in the asylum.

Rhian's elbow sank into Garrick's ribs.

He nodded. "Yeah, I see it."

Reese, who had become increasingly comfortable when visiting Garrick at home, was clearly overwhelmed by the noise and crowd in the bar. Garrick approached slowly.

"Gentlemen," he said loud enough to be heard over the din.

Reese spun around like he'd been goosed. He tried hard to come up with a smile but only managed a painful grimace.

Rupert appeared downright alarmed. "We should go."

"No." Reese sounded like he meant it, even if he looked like he wanted to run screaming.

Garrick glanced back at Rhian at the bar, not surprised he was watching the drama unfold, then searched the restaurant and found just what he needed. He turned to the hostess. "Can we sit about ten of us in the back, Sandy?"

She beamed up at him. "Sure, Garrick. Take forty-three. The booth and whatever tables you need next to it."

He pointed to the quiet corner of the room and smiled at Reese. "Would that help?"

Reese leaped on that plan like a drowning man, nodding quickly.

"Okay, then," Garrick said brightly while shooting Rupert a look.

Rupert shrugged.

Reese edged past them and fixed his sights on their quiet table.

Garrick caught Rupert's arm before he could follow. "When was the last time he went out like this?"

Rupert watched Reese closely while he answered. "I'm not sure. It's been a few years, at least."

"Did you say *years*?"

Rupert looked back at him. "Did you miss the part where you went into business with a famous recluse?"

"No, I, uh… I just figured he'd been faking it. He showed up here in Moncton not long after we met."

"And it was the first time he'd left Nova Scotia in five years. Maybe only the tenth time he'd left his property in the past twelve months."

"Holy shit."

Before Rupert could respond, Alexei came up and threw a huge arm around Rupert's shoulder, almost knocking him off his feet. "Boss! I'm so glad you came out with us tonight."

Rupert staggered in an attempt to remain upright. "I uh…yes, well, thank you very much for inviting me to join you."

Garrick shot Alexei a look then pointedly stared at his arm until he backed off. He knew Alexei wasn't trying to frighten Rupert so much as figure out what the hell made him so jumpy. Alexei was probably learning fast, since he was succeeding in pushing all Rupert's buttons. Rupert became painfully polite and prim when he was nervous or upset, and the fact that he was as white as a sheet was hard to miss.

Rhian and the rest of the guys caught up to them halfway across the restaurant. They made it to the table in one piece and Garrick made introductions, suppressing a sudden case of Tourette syndrome that made him want to scream, "This is Edwin Lamont!" They shook hands all around, then sat. Garrick ended up somewhere in the middle, pressed tightly to Rhian— just where he wanted to be—with Rupert and Reese sitting in the corner on Rhian's other side.

They'd no sooner settled into their seats when the conversation turned to the team and Justin's trade. He was headed to some team in Bumfuck, Saskatchewan and everyone was going on and on about how sorry they felt for him and his family.

Garrick wished the floor would open up and swallow him whole. What the fuck had he been thinking, setting this up? He should be home working, not pretending that every one of his teammates—except Rhian, by some miracle—wasn't going to fucking hate him.

He fought like hell to keep his face blank, not even wincing at Rupert and Rhian's blatant and unsuccessful attempts to steer the conversation elsewhere. The only thing that made Garrick feel better was Rhian's leg wrapped around his under the table, the steady pressure a constant reminder of his support.

Garrick sat silently while the conversation slowly gutted him, ignoring Rhian's furiously whispered exchange with Rupert. He couldn't imagine what the hell the two of them were discussing.

When Tim, Dave, and Chris went to the bar to get another

round for the table, Rhian shoved against him, forcing him out of the booth.

"Where are you going?" Garrick asked, squashing his panic that Rhian was leaving him alone. He wondered where the hell he'd left his big-boy pants. Jesus.

"We're going to the bathroom. Come on." Rhian walked away without checking to see if he followed.

Garrick trailed after him like a dutiful girlfriend who wouldn't leave her sister-in-arms to pee alone. He could only imagine what the hell the guys thought about this.

It was a damn good thing no one was in the hallway to see Rhian shove him into the unisex handicap bathroom and lock the door behind them.

Rhian might be the sexiest man Garrick had ever laid eyes on—let alone lips and hands—but no way in hell was Garrick up for getting it on in the bar bathroom tonight. It wasn't a matter of principle. Hell no. It was a matter of feeling like dog crap about keeping this stupid fucking secret. He couldn't get it up if he tried.

Rhian folded his arms across his chest and stared Garrick down.

Guess they weren't here to get freaky after all.

"You need to tell them."

Garrick shook his head. "I can't."

"Yes, you can. According to Rupert, you can tell anyone you want that you're one of the new owners—you're just not allowed to tell them who the others are. You *have* to tell them. You can't pretend this isn't awful."

Simultaneously touched and humiliated, Garrick started to protest that he was fine, but Rhian's hand on his cheek stalled the words.

Rhian was right. This was fucking killing him.

"I can't tell them. Not now."

"Why not?"

The concern in Rhian's voice was almost his undoing, but his pride would never survive crying in the Quigley's Bar and Grill lavatory. He swallowed hard. "I don't want to make a scene."

"What scene? Why would there be a scene?"

"They're going to be pissed. I'll be lucky if all they do is get up and leave."

"I don't get it, Garrick. Everyone out there has been traded at least once. They know how it works."

They didn't have families. A little girl who would miss her friends. Who might be angry with her father for something he couldn't control.

Garrick had done the right thing, what he'd needed to do. But he didn't want to see the guys' faces when they learned he'd gone from being their friend to the man who could—and would, if he had to—send them away.

Their boss.

He was, he accepted with a tired shrug, a complete chickenshit.

He didn't look at Rhian when he unlocked the door and headed for the table.

Alexei's booming laugh carried to him across the room and Garrick looked up to see everyone watched them approach. He slapped a smile on his face and slid into the booth behind Rhian, who promptly wrapped his calf around Garrick's shin again.

The conversation swirled around him while he counted the minutes until he could go home. All he wanted was call Savannah, tell her he loved her, then curl into bed with as many parts of his body pressed to as many of Rhian's as he could manage.

They believed in him. Had never so much as blinked in their faith that Garrick had done the right thing. And soon they'd *both* be several hundred miles away.

Garrick turned to Rhian and spoke softly, so only he could

hear. "I'm going to miss you."

Rhian's lips parted and he blinked a few times before he looked at Garrick. Garrick turned back to the table. This wasn't the time, or the place. And hell, he probably shouldn't have said it anyway, but he'd needed to. He wanted Rhian to know.

It wasn't long before the subject returned to the new owners and Justin's trade, yet again. Rhian didn't try to change the subject. Neither did Rupert. Or Reese.

"Wait." The word left Garrick's mouth before he'd really accepted what he was about to do.

Everyone looked at him. Rhian smiled encouragingly. Hell, so did Rupert.

"I'm one of the new owners of the Ice Cats. I'm one of the partners."

Absolute silence fell over the table. No one moved, except Rhian, whose leg tightening against Garrick's, pressing his calf to the booth. It was his only anchor.

Chris was the first to break the shocked silence. "Are you fucking serious?"

"Yes," Garrick said, his voice calm in spite of the tug of nausea in his gut. He remembered all the shit they'd slung about the new owners in front of him. Judging by the looks on their faces, they were recalling the same thing. Too bad there was no going back. "I'm sorry I didn't tell you sooner. I didn't realize…" Hell, he hadn't realized a lot of things. That the deal would take this long to finalize. That he'd feel like such an asshole. That he'd have to send their friend to fucking Saskatchewan.

"You're *sorry*?" Tim asked.

Dave stared at Garrick, his face red. "Dude, what the fuck?"

Chris and Dave jumped to their feet. Tim rose more slowly.

"Where are you going?" Rhian demanded.

Garrick slammed a hand on Rhian's arm to keep him in his seat. Regret churned in his stomach.

"Home," Chris grunted. "I'm suddenly not in the mood to

celebrate." He sent Garrick a look that made him feel like Zamboni sludge, then nodded to Rhian. "Congratulations, man."

Then he left. Dave followed him without a word. Tim watched them go before looking back at Garrick.

"Sorry, man. You just…you surprised us."

Garrick nodded.

"Anyway, ummm…" Tim hesitated, waving over his shoulder. "Dave's my ride. I gotta go."

"Sure." Garrick hardly recognized the dull voice as his own.

He watched Tim weave through the tables, then finally found the balls to face Mike and Alexei.

Garrick almost jumped out of his seat when Alexei's huge hand pounded on the table, their glasses rattling. "This explains why you've had a giant hockey stick up your ass for last month, no?"

Garrick ignored the loud guffaw from Reese.

"Pardon me?"

Mike smiled ruefully. "What he's trying to say," he began, blatantly kicking his friend's shin under the table, "is that we'd noticed you'd been acting differently."

Alexei glared at Mike. "What? This is what I said."

Garrick's lips twitched, tempted toward a smile, but he knew the worst was yet to come. He might as well get it all out on the table. "You have to understand. I'm the one who traded Justin."

Alexei cocked his head. "This was a good decision?"

"It was."

Mike pursed his lips. "Sucks, huh?"

Garrick hesitated. "Yeah."

"And this decision, you made it because you want Justin gone and are a total asshole? Or because it is best for the team?" Alexei asked.

Rhian grinned, his eyes shining with *I told you so*.

Garrick slumped back in his seat and took a long pull from

his beer, all the while shooting Alexei a dirty look. "It's best for the team, of course."

"And your partners, they let you make decisions without them? Without Rupert here?"

"No, of course not."

"And Lamont, he is an idiot?"

No one appeared more interested in his answer than Reese, who cocked one brow and stared at Garrick with a big smile.

Garrick's lips twitched. "No, of course not. But I made the decision."

Alexei nodded once. "Okay."

"Okay?"

"Yeah, okay. And congratulations. You going to keep skating?"

"No. I'm retiring at the end of the season."

"That's a shame." Mike shook Garrick's hand. "Congrats, though."

"Uh, thanks."

Mike leaned in. "So, can I ask a question?"

"Uh...sure. What's that?"

"What's it like working with that crazy old coot Lamont?"

Rupert choked on an ill-timed sip of ale as Reese's booming laugh rang out over the crowd.

Garrick found he had a genuine smile, in spite of what had happened that night. "Let's just say he's not at all who you expect him to be."

Chapter Twenty One

Rhian shifted against the hard seat of his car, acutely aware of the sting in his ass every time he moved, but unable to sit still. It wasn't that it was uncomfortable. The issue was more that he loved it.

Jesus, he was turning into a slut.

Last night they'd left the bar within five minutes of each other so Rhian could chase Garrick back to his house. He'd barely made it in the door before Garrick was tearing his clothes off, their headlong stumble toward the stairs only getting as far as the dining room before Garrick, who had apparently planned for just such an eventuality, bent him over the dining room table, shoved two lubed fingers up his ass, and stretched his eager muscles just enough to accommodate Garrick's thick cock.

Rhian had ended up with one knee on the table top, spread wide and begging. A grunt had burst from him with every hard thrust, his hands skittering across the high-gloss surface for enough purchase to hold still while Garrick made them both howl.

The sex had been phenomenal. Garrick had wrapped himself around Rhian and whispered "thank you, thank you, thank you," with every deep thrust, pounding his gratitude into Rhian. He could only nod and moan until his climax had wiped his mind of everything but the intense satisfaction, the joy, of that moment.

A shiver ran down the back of his neck when he recalled the cool touch of wood against his cheek, while the ever-present ache in his ass zinged up his spine. He'd never been so *sated* in his life.

The only black spot on the entire night was Chris, Dave, and Tim's reactions to Garrick's confession. That had not gone down the way Rhian had thought it would. He intended to have a serious talk with those guys as soon as he could find them and a private place to speak. That shit could not stand, and he didn't have much time to help them pull their heads from their asses before he left Moncton for good.

He shook off another wave of sadness as pulled into the arena parking lot for his last game with the Moncton Ice Cats, trying to figure out when he'd started to think of this city as his home.

How the fuck was he going to get the old Rhian back? He had to find that guy, and fast. The one who didn't believe in attachments. Always ready to move on to the next gig. One hundred percent focused on hockey.

The NHL was his dream, and it was coming true. That was the most important thing. The brass ring. Everything he did *had* to revolve around meeting that goal.

Rhian looked up to see Garrick's truck roaring into the lot. He climbed out of his car, waving to grab Garrick's attention, but Garrick was already running for the arena. He hadn't planned to come in for another hour, so something sure as hell was wrong.

Rhian took off after him and barreled through the lobby door right on Garrick's heels.

Garrick ran faster.

What the fuck is going on?

They ended up at Rupert's office. Garrick tried to slam the door in Rhian's face, but Rhian wasn't having it. He needed to know Garrick was all right. He wedged his foot against the door, forced his way in, and shut it firmly behind him.

Rupert jumped to his feet.

Garrick spun on Rhian. "Get out."

Rhian pressed his back to the door. "What happened?"

"*Get out*, Rhian. I don't want you anywhere near me."

Rhian felt like he'd been slammed to the boards without his helmet. His lungs locked up, all the air forced out. "*What?*"

Garrick immediately relented and pressed a hand to his

cheek. "No, baby. I don't mean..." He stopped and sighed. "Shit, since you're in here, you might as well hear it."

"Hear what?"

Garrick didn't say anything, just stood there staring at him.

Rupert finally found his voice. "One Deena Lewis called the league this morning. She claims Garrick raped her last night after leaving the bar."

The blood drained from Rhian's head and his knees buckled. He slid down the door and landed on his ass with a thump.

Garrick turned away and began pacing in the small office like a caged lion.

"It's a fucking lie," Rhian croaked from the floor.

"Of course it is," Rupert snapped. He turned to Garrick. "What are you going to do? Do you have an alibi?"

Garrick glared at Rhian. "No. No alibi." It wasn't a statement, it was a command.

Rhian sat up. "Garrick—"

"No! I have no fucking alibi."

Garrick spun in the tight space. He wanted to punch the wall and then wipe the contents of Rupert's desk onto the floor. Rupert would probably wet himself if Garrick did.

Overwhelmed with frustration, he seethed silently and paced maniacally.

Rhian couldn't alibi him. He was leaving for Boston in two days. *Two fucking days.* Garrick would not be the reason that fell through. He had no fucking idea how he was going to get out from under this bullshit, but it would not be at Rhian's expense.

Rhian looked stricken. God, Garrick fucking hated that. He looked away. He wanted to apologize for yelling, but right now the words were beyond him.

Fisting his hands in his hair, he turned to Rupert for

support and froze. Rupert stood with his back to the far corner of his office, putting as much space between himself and Garrick as possible, his face pale and eyes wide.

He looked absolutely terrified.

"Jesus, Rupert. I'm not going to hurt you!"

Rupert nodded. His eyes never left Garrick's face.

Battling his desire to yell that now was not the time for Rupert's issues to explode all over them, Garrick collected himself and tried to appear less threatening.

"I'm not going to hurt you," he said again in as calm a voice as he could manage.

"I know." The quickly blurted words were not convincing.

"Rupert, please. Help me." Garrick was shocked at how raw his voice, his plea, came out.

Rupert stepped up to his desk, though still kept it between them. "I will help you. Of course. I'll call Reese. And the others. They need to be told. And you need to prepare your response. You need an alibi."

Garrick glanced at Rhian again and swallowed. "I don't have an alibi."

Rhian opened his mouth to say something, but Garrick cut him off. "No, Rhian. Please. I would never forgive myself."

Rupert cleared his throat. "Can you at least tell me?"

Garrick sighed and turned back to Rupert. "Rhian and I went to my house from the bar last night. He was with me all night."

"But that's good," Rupert said, so fucking hopeful.

"No, it's not. We're not going to tell anyone that. If you tell anyone, Rupert, I'm going to deny it. And so will Rhian."

Rhian stood.

"I have no alibi," Garrick said one last time. Firmly. "We're going to have to figure out another way to prove Deena is a crazy fucking liar."

Rupert looked between the two of them. Garrick refused to

glance at Rhian. They both knew this was the right thing to do.

Rupert nodded slowly and sat down at his desk. "Okay, that's going to be a problem, but let's figure out what else we can do."

Rhian collapsed into one of Rupert's guest chairs. "She can't have any proof. Maybe someone saw her wherever she really went last night."

"I never saw her at the bar," Garrick said. "Did either of you see her?"

Rupert shrugged. "I don't know who this creature is, so I wouldn't know."

Rhian shook his head. "I didn't see her. Or any of her friends. We can ask the rest of the guys."

That would be Garrick's first stop when he left here. He wasn't looking forward to hearing whatever else Tim, Dave, and Chris might want to say to him.

Fuck. He'd worry about that later. He had to focus on the big shit right now. "The rest of the team went to Smitty's, and presumably the puck bunnies and fans went there, too."

"Except that one fellow," Rupert said. "The one who likes to watch you practice, Rhian."

Rhian went rigid in his seat.

Garrick's head snapped up. "Who?"

"You know the one. He likes to sit in the stands during practice. He watches Rhian like a hawk. I'd wondered if he was a scout who hadn't heard Rhian had already been signed to Boston."

Garrick's blood went cold. "Steve."

Rhian slumped, his face in his hands. "Oh god, Garrick. I'm so sorry."

Garrick growled. "Shut up. It's not your fault." He turned back to Rupert. "Where was he?"

"What?" Once again Rupert was looking between them, clearly wanting to ask questions.

Too bad. Garrick wasn't going to tell him about the blackmail and he wasn't about to let Rhian do it either.

"Where and when did you see Steve?" Garrick repeated. "Rhian's fan," he clarified through gritted teeth.

Rupert shrugged. "When Reese and I were leaving. He was in the booth next to ours."

Garrick began to grasp the sheer size and velocity of the shit storm they were in. "Fuck," he muttered. "He heard me tell everyone I'm an owner." He looked at Rhian. "It doesn't matter. He thinks by coming after me, he's punishing you. Forcing your hand. But if you alibi me, he'll really have you by the short hairs."

Rhian swallowed so hard his throat clicked. "God, I'm so sorry. I'll find him. Give him whatever he wants."

"No, you won't. That's a fucking rat hole and you know it. And it wouldn't fix anything. He still knows all kinds of shit he shouldn't and he can't be trusted. We're better off discrediting Deena. Though, the chances of us finding someone else who saw Deena last night are slim. I'm just going to have to hope the cops see through it."

"Garrick," Rhian pleaded, "Maybe I can—"

"You *can't.*"

Rhian couldn't stop this. Not without risking everything. The Bruins had nothing invested at this point. No way would they put up with any kind of scandal or police investigation. They'd drop Rhian's ass like a hot potato if they got even a whiff of trouble. As far as the Bruins were concerned, Rhian was expendable.

"Garrick," Rupert said thoughtfully, "have the police contacted you?"

"No. Not yet."

Rupert pulled something up on his monitor. "This says Deena contacted the league. Not Ice Cats management. I suppose that goes to your supposition that she knows you're one of the new owners."

Garrick nodded, not sure where Rupert was going.

"But why," Rupert continued, "wouldn't she have gone to the police?"

"Because it's bullshit?" Rhian said.

"Yes, of course, but I'm wondering what she really wants. Why call the league? Why not the police?"

"She wants something," Garrick agreed. "I'm fairly certain she's not acting on her own. I'm almost positive Steve is putting her up to it."

"Why?" Rupert asked again.

Garrick glanced at Rhian's guilty face. "It doesn't matter. I just need to figure out how to stop it."

"Should *you* go to the police?" Rupert asked.

Garrick mulled that over. "I'm not sure I want to put myself on their radar. It's not going to go well for the team and the rest of the owners if I start spreading this shit around."

"Garrick, my friend," Rupert said drily, "this shit is spreading faster than you can stop it. Maybe you should report her first. Offer your DNA. Fingerprints. Whatever."

It wasn't a bad idea. Garrick stood. "I want to talk to Jack. He's got a friend who's a Mountie. Maybe Jack can get him to talk to me off the record. See what he suggests."

"Good idea," Rupert said.

Rhian rose to his feet. "I'll come with you."

"No," Garrick said, wincing at his sharp tone. The hurt on Rhian's face was fucking killing him. "Rupert, pull me from the roster. Let Rick know I'm off the ice, possibly for good."

Rhian appeared more upset by his request than Garrick felt.

"Please, Rhian. Walk out of this office and don't look back. Go to the gym. Kick ass in tonight's game. Go home. Pack. From now on, I don't exist."

"But—"

"You have to stay clear of this. Of me. Do you understand?

You leave in two days. Just fucking hold your breath and get it done. You can't have anything to do with me."

It was the right thing to do, the best possible outcome, the unavoidable result they'd been planning on all along.

The end.

Only Garrick hadn't planned on it hurting so damn much.

Rhian looked like he wanted to argue. In fact, he looked furious. "Fuck you," he whispered hoarsely.

Then he was gone, the door slamming behind him.

Chapter Twenty Two

Rhian sat at the bar in Smitty's, surrounded by post-win hockey revelers getting drunk and stupid. But then, who was he to judge? He was the stupidest of them all to even be there.

He scanned the crowd again and felt a jolt of fury when he saw Deena coming through the door. She looked like hell. Another black eye, her cheek scraped raw, and her chin badly bruised.

Jesus Christ, she claimed Garrick had done that?

Clearly someone *had* attacked her, and Rhian didn't have to guess who. Fucking Steve. How could he do that to someone?

Forcing thoughts of Steve, who was nowhere to be found, out of his mind, he kept an eye on Deena. He left her to mingle for a while, waiting until she'd spoken to at least ten other people who would be able to verify she was drinking and having a grand old time, soaking up all the attention her injuries garnered. Dave and Chris studied her face, their concern obvious. She laughed it off and flirted so aggressively, his friends looked alarmed by her behavior. Rhian almost smiled. They may have been total assholes last night, but Rhian still believed Garrick could count on them to stand by him when push came to shove.

And Deena was giving Garrick one hell of a shove.

When he couldn't stand to wait another minute, he stood from his seat in the thick of the crowd and moved to Deena's side.

"You have a minute?" he asked quietly over her shoulder.

She spun around, and he got a closer look at her face, wincing in spite of his anger. Steve had really worked her over.

"What the fuck do *you* want?" she said, way too loudly.

Rhian forced a smile, nodding at the guys before turning back to Deena. "Let's talk. Over here where everyone can see us."

She studied him, eventually shrugging. Rhian led the way to the side of the room, still in the bar but away from prying ears.

Tim had joined Chris and Dave, and Rhian was painfully aware of their curious gazes.

"Let me help you, Deena. You can't let Steve use you like this."

It wasn't what he'd intended to say when he'd come looking for her, but he couldn't help but see her as a victim when he took in the damage.

"Fuck you, Savage." She turned to walk away, but he caught her arm.

Rhian gritted his teeth. God, she was stupid. "What do you want?"

"Pardon me?"

"What do you want, Deena? I know you don't want help, but there has to be something you want. Money? Sex?" Not that he could go through with the sex if she took him up on it. The very idea made him ill.

"Sex?" she asked with a strident laugh. "You think I want to fuck you now, you perv? I've seen what you like, and it's sick."

He almost puked at the thought that she'd seen anything of the sort. Holy shit, *did* Steve have proof?

"Money, then?"

Deena hooted, the sound grating across his nerves. "God, look at you. Groveling for your fag lover. You'd actually fuck me because you love him? Jesus, that's priceless."

Rhian winced, praying her shrill voice didn't carry over the music and loud conversations to the people around them.

"We both know you're lying, Deena. You can't have any proof that Garrick attacked you. What are you going to do when the cops ask for evidence?"

Her eyes widened at the mention of the police, but she

recovered quickly. "Fuck you. They'll believe me if I tell them it's true. We have a plan and it's working perfectly. Look at you here, pleading with me. I can't wait to tell him about this."

Either her voice was getting louder or his panic was making his hearing more acute. They were dangerously close to making a scene. With a sinking heart, he stared down at the hatred, the insanity, shining in Deena's face. He'd made a mistake coming here.

Without another word, he turned and left the bar.

Garrick sat in his kitchen and stared at the empty coffee cups Jack and his friend Grady had left behind. He felt fortunate Jack had been willing to call in a favor, and that Grady, a member of the RCMP, had been willing to come out to the house.

He was pretty sure Jack had doubted his claim of being home alone last night. Garrick was a notoriously terrible liar, but he'd sold it for all he was worth. Jack, thank god, hadn't questioned him.

Grady hadn't had much in the way of encouraging news or suggestions. If it boiled down to a he-said-she-said, he could be in some serious shit. His guts churned at the idea that Deena and Steve could destroy him. But he'd be damned if they would take Rhian down with him.

Cleaning up the kitchen, he tried to empty his mind of everything but the next incredibly grim task at hand. The call to Savannah. How the hell was he going to tell her?

He dragged his ass upstairs, stripped, and crawled into bed with his cell phone. It was late and he could feel exhaustion pulling him under.

With a sigh, he dialed Savannah's number.

"Hello, stranger."

Her voice, as always, warmed him.

"Hi there."

"What's wrong?"

He appreciated that she didn't beat around the bush, and he hadn't kept the sadness, the resignation from his voice. There was no way to pretty this up.

"I've got a problem. A big one." He laid it all out. Deena's accusation. His lack of alibi, and why. He wasn't going to lie to Savannah about any of it. He trusted her to understand.

Savannah was outraged, furious, frustrated. All the things he was experiencing. It was hard not to let fear overrule everything else, but she worked her way past it the way he had been doing all day. He told her about his conversation with Jack and Grady. If Deena went to the cops, he would immediately turn himself in to try to get out in front of this thing.

"What are you going to tell them?" she asked.

"I don't know. That it's bullshit? That I don't have any way of proving that it's bullshit, except that I'm certain she can't have any proof either?"

"Garrick, maybe you should talk to Rhian. Maybe—"

"No."

"Is he asking you not to tell anyone?"

"No, nothing like that. Hell, he'd do it. He'd fucking ruin his career if I let him. That's why I can't. Sav, I don't know how to explain it, but he needs protecting. He needs to go to Boston and have his dreams come true. He's got so much promise, and not just on the ice. And this innate dignity. Like you, actually. He would toss it all away to help me, but I can't let him. I want his dreams to come true, too, you know? Maybe that sounds stupid."

There was a long pause, and for a moment Garrick worried his cell phone had cut out.

"*Oh my god,*" Savannah said, shock thick in her voice. "*You're in love with him.*"

"What? No." His heart squeezed painfully in his chest at the denial. "I love *you.*"

When she didn't answer, he panicked, barely able to

breathe, his eyes burning.

"Savannah, please. I love you. You know I do. You have to believe me. My feelings for you have not changed. At all."

The next ten seconds were the longest of his entire fucking life.

"I believe you," she said at last.

He slumped on the bed. "Thank god," he murmured, wiping the tears from his cheeks. "I love you, baby. I do. I want to spend the rest of my life proving that to you. I'm one hundred percent certain about that."

"I believe you," she said again, this time with more conviction. "But tell me something, Garrick."

"Yeah?" He dreaded what would come next. No one could see through him like Savannah.

"How do you feel about never seeing him again? About never being with him again? Never touching him. Holding him."

Garrick fought to breathe past the steel band around his chest. He wanted to lie. To tell her he felt nothing, that it was cool and had been fun and he was totally fine that it was over. But he couldn't.

"Sad," he confessed in a soft voice. "But..."

"Have you changed the way you act around him? Have *you* changed?"

"It hasn't changed the way I feel about you."

"I believe you. But tell me the truth. What's changed?"

He thought about it for a while, trying to find the right words. "He makes me more...patient, I guess. I mean, you know I'm not normally a patient person. I want to demand answers to all these mysteries he's carrying around, but I can't. I won't, because I know it would hurt him to tell me before he's ready. And I don't ever want him to be hurt. I want to protect him. I want to prove to him that someone out there will do the right thing. Will put him first. God, Savannah, I don't think anyone has ever put him first."

"So you want to save him?"

"No, that's not it," he countered, trying to figure it out as he was saying it. "He makes me want to be the kind of person he deserves to be with. A better person, maybe, than I am now."

Savannah was quiet for a moment.

"Do you hear yourself?" she asked gently.

"Jesus, I—"

"Garrick, I don't know what this means, but let's not lie to ourselves or each other about it. How could we possibly build our lives together if we do that?"

"I do want to build a life with you." His voice had gone hideously hoarse.

"I want that, too. And we will."

"I love you. I love you so much. I never meant to hurt you."

"I am hurt," she admitted softly.

A boulder settled in Garrick's chest. He couldn't have gotten words past the constriction in his throat, even if he'd known what the fuck to say.

"And I'm worried" she continued. "But to be honest, I'm more confused than anything else."

"I hear that," he muttered.

"We'll figure this out, Garrick. But in the meantime, don't lie to yourself. Or to Rhian."

"I can't..."

"You can't go anywhere near him for now. I agree. But in a few months, you'll both be in Boston, and then what?"

He'd been certain he knew the answer minutes ago. *And then nothing.* That might still be the answer, but the fact Savannah even asked the question, without censure or anger or judgment, was nothing short of miraculous.

"How the hell did I get so fucking lucky and find you?" he asked, swallowing against the lump in his throat.

"Because you're the kind of person *I* deserve."

Her soft words brought a smile and a wave of relief. He would figure this out. *They* would figure this out. But before he could think about the future, he had a very grim present to deal with. Christ, how the hell was he going to get to Boston, to Savannah, with a bogus rape charge hanging over his head?

What if they told him he couldn't leave town? Leave the country? Suddenly, the genius of Steve's fucked-up plan became crystal clear. Rhian gets to the NHL, Steve gets his blackmail money, and Garrick is trapped in New Brunswick without a team to own or play for, for which Rhian would never forgive himself.

Son of a bitch.

Chapter Twenty Three

Garrick lay awake in bed hours later. His mind churned over his situation, trying to come up with a way to stop Deena and Steve. He refused to look at the clock, knowing only a few minutes had passed since the last time he'd checked. Confirming he was wide awake at three in the morning wasn't going to make him feel any better. Or help him sleep.

The house was quiet, without so much as the creaks and groans the wind could pull from the antique frame and clapboard. Even Mother Nature seemed to be holding her breath, waiting to see what would happen next.

He startled when he heard the distant but distinct squeak of his kitchen door opening.

It could be burglars. His luck was just about that shitty right now. Or the police, coming to get him. Or Deena, hoping to entrap him. Or Steve. That last thought was the only one that truly worried him. But none of those people knew where he hid his key.

He was hardly surprised when Rhian appeared in his bedroom doorway, shucking his clothes as he crossed the room. Garrick wanted to yell at him, to throw him out. He should have done both. But he just lay there in mute fascination as his heartbeat picked up, his belly warmed, and he stopped denying all the signals he'd been studiously ignoring as they worked their way through his body.

He was so screwed.

Rhian stopped next to the bed and stared down at him. "I couldn't sleep," he admitted quietly.

Garrick lifted the covers. Rhian slid in and rolled toward Garrick without hesitation. Their lips met. Their legs and arms twined to bring each other closer.

Garrick wasn't used to the Rhian who came easily into his embrace. It had been days, and he was still surprised. Felt a little awe, every time. He thought about what he'd told Savannah and wondered if he was the kind of man Rhian deserved.

And what did it say about Rhian's feeling toward him that Rhian welcomed his touch, this quiet intimacy, in a way he'd been incapable of only a week ago?

He shied away from that thought, afraid to know the answer. He could be some grand experiment. A fling. It was all they'd ever agreed to, after all.

He scraped his fingers over Rhian's scalp and cupped the back of his head, enjoying the soft brush of silk. Rhian opened beneath his lips and he delved into the hot recesses of Rhian's mouth, tasting the lingering hint of toothpaste.

Big hands dug into Garrick's back, strong arms holding so tightly he fought to breathe. It was perfect. He wanted to be held like this, almost desperately. He wanted Rhian to cling to him the way he was trying to wrap himself around Rhian. Like he might never let go. Like he could keep him forever.

Rolling, he pressed Rhian's back to the bed and reveled in Rhian's acquiescence, the way their tongues danced together, the way Rhian's hold didn't loosen even as he melted beneath Garrick.

For the first time since he'd thrown Rhian out of Rupert's office and—he'd believed—his bed, Garrick felt something akin to calm. The worries were still there, the fear about what would come tomorrow, but the taste of Rhian on his lips, Rhian's hard body beneath his, soothed him.

Rhian shouldn't have risked coming here, let alone in the middle of the night, but Garrick wasn't sorry. He would never be sorry about any of it.

Rhian drew his legs up around Garrick's hips. Garrick shuddered. It felt like Rhian was trying to pull him right into his body. Their kisses edged toward frantic. He curled one hand around Rhian's hip. Rhian cupped both hands over his ass.

Lightheaded from the blood rushing through his veins and

a lack of oxygen, Garrick tore his mouth from Rhian's. He worked his way across Rhian's morning beard to his jaw, behind his ear, and down his neck. His lips fastened over corded muscles and sucked a moan up from deep inside Rhian's chest, the only sound to interrupt the rough saw of his breath.

Garrick grabbed a condom and lube from the bedside table, his mouth never leaving Rhian's shoulder, his chest. His hands shook, but he managed to prepare them both, all the while worshiping whatever parts of Rhian he could reach with his mouth.

Chest. Biceps. The palm of the hand that came to rest on Garrick's cheek.

He looked up to find Rhian staring at him with clear blue eyes.

He lodged the head of his cock against the entrance to Rhian's ass and stared back, rubbing his cheek against the hand still holding his face.

They should not be here. Doing this. The risks were enormous, and only some of them had to do with Steve and his plans to punish Rhian.

But the heart wants what it wants.

Without breaking their locked gazes, Garrick eased forward and sank all the way into Rhian's beautiful body.

Rhian knew he should keep what he was feeling, what he was thinking, off his face, but he couldn't be bothered. As the heavy thrust of Garrick's cock stretched him open, he bit his lip and fought the need to close his eyes against the wave of bliss rushing up from where they were joined.

This was it. *One last time*, he promised himself as he took a deep breath and relaxed, allowing Garrick to come another centimeter closer. This was what he'd wanted. Needed so badly he'd driven out here in the middle of the night rather than lie awake, denying it any longer.

He slid his thumb over Garrick's cheekbone and wondered what his friend was thinking. He stared at Rhian with those deep brown eyes like he'd never seen him before. Perhaps confused. Or sad.

Rhian wouldn't ask. He didn't really want to know. They both understood this was goodbye. It had to be.

He curled up to meet Garrick's mouth, their kiss slow and erotic, their circling tongues mimicking the slow rotation of Garrick's hips. He wasn't thrusting so much as grinding himself as deeply into Rhian as he could get. Exactly where Rhian wanted him.

They stayed like that for a long time, slowly easing down until Rhian's head rested on the bed and he was covered by Garrick's broad body and comforting weight. He slid his hands into Garrick's hair and lifted his legs higher, easing the awkwardness of the position and inviting Garrick to move.

Rhian needed him to move. He needed to do more than lie there and kiss Garrick while he was buried to the hilt in Rhian's body, or he might never leave. He had to leave. He had to go to Boston and never look back.

Garrick lifted his hips and let them fall again slowly, gently. Over and over. Rhian kept expecting him to pick up speed, increase the intensity and depth of his thrusts as he'd done in the past, but he didn't, damn him. Rhian kissed him harder, squeezing his eyes shut against the burn building behind his lids.

He would not embarrass himself, or Garrick, that way.

Garrick shifted, and on the next thrust he hit that sweet spot deep in Rhian's body. Their kiss ended only for the length of Rhian's gasp. The next thrust, the next burst of pleasure, was swallowed by Garrick's mouth, licked up on his tongue.

Rhian rode the waves, his cock a steel bar against Garrick's belly, leaving a trail of moisture as it rolled over the hard ridges of muscle. Garrick kept to his steady, maddening pace as Rhian climbed to the brink of some cliff, one he was desperate to hurl himself from and yet wouldn't as long as he could hold onto this feeling. To Garrick.

At last he dove off, the tight muscles in his ass clenching fiercely around Garrick's cock. Their lips parted on a mutual gasp, Rhian's back bowing as Garrick shuddered above him. The clockwork snap of Garrick's hips drew out Rhian's pleasure, the quiet grunt of his name on Garrick's lips drawing his eyes open to enjoy the shocked ecstasy on Garrick's face.

He'd been right to come here, to take this last memory with him. He caught Garrick's weight and pulled him to his chest.

He held on while they both caught their breath, biting his lip and suppressing his moan of disappointment when Garrick slid from his body for the last time. Garrick disposed of the condom, then rolled onto his side and pulled Rhian against him in their now familiar set of spoons.

Garrick would normally help Rhian clean up, a ritual that had once embarrassed the hell out of Rhian but which he'd learned to appreciate. Neither moved to do it now. Garrick's breathing turned slow and even, the once-strong hold around Rhian's ribs going lax as Garrick slid into a deep sleep.

Rhian lay there, unmoving, and stared at the picture of Savannah on the bedside table until he feared dawn was coming. Then he slid out of the bed, into his clothes, and out of the house.

Chapter Twenty Four

Garrick woke after a few short hours of sleep and told himself he was neither surprised nor disappointed to find Rhian was gone. It was for the best.

He dragged his ass out of bed and took a stinging hot shower—a failed attempt at reinvigoration. He would have complained about how little sleep he'd gotten, but in truth, if Rhian hadn't come over, he would have been up all night. All in all, a racking orgasm and four hours of sleep wasn't bad.

Now he just had to convince the league, and possibly the police, that he wasn't a rapist and he'd be all set.

Right.

He went to the arena first. He wanted to tell Rupert his intentions, if for no other reason than he might need bailing out and there was no way in hell he was going to call his mother or sister. And since Savannah was in Boston and Rhian was forbidden to acknowledge his existence, Rupert and Reese seemed like his best bets.

A commotion echoed down the corridor from the direction of the gym and locker room. Garrick made his way around the curved passage, stuttering to a stop when Rupert, Reese, the entire Moncton Ice Cats team, and four of Moncton's finest came into view. Badges flashed in the fluorescent lighting, two winking from the chests of the uniformed officers, the others from the belts of the plain-clothes detectives.

"He did nothing of the sort!" Rupert yelled, remarkably brazen in the face of the youngest and shortest detective.

"Sir, I appreciate you don't believe the charges levied against your friend, but we still need to speak with him. Do you know where we can find Garrick LeBlanc?" He enunciated the question, obviously having asked it before.

Garrick's first instinct was to run. In a choice between fight or flight, flight seemed like a better option when he had to enter the fight with nothing but the truth and no alibi.

A voice came from the crowd. "There he is!"

Bodies shifted to look at the traitor, revealing Steve and Deena hidden amongst the players.

The cops turned to Garrick, and he held his hands out in front of himself in the hopes of keeping everyone calm. He'd planned to go to the cops if it came to this. He just hadn't planned on an audience. Had someone sent out invitations?

As if on cue, Jack ran up behind him. "I just heard. Stay cool, man. We're going to fix this."

Garrick tried to smile at his friend, the ex-con who'd done a five-year stint in prison for being a dumb and confused kid. Not a lot of reassurance there.

He continued toward the crowd and the cops. "Officers, I'm glad you're here. I'll cooperate however you need me to. I want to clear my name." He spoke in a strong, level voice. Heads nodded. In particular, his coach, Rick, appeared approving, and for some damn reason, this lent him confidence.

The detective Rupert had been shouting at turned suspicious eyes on him. "Garrick LeBlanc?"

"Yes."

"We need you to come with us, sir."

"Okay. Tell me what you need. I want to help."

"And why is that?" the detective asked with what passed as humor, but reeked of cynicism.

"Because I didn't do it." The crowd shifted and he caught a glimpse of Deena's delighted smirk. "Because I'm determined to prove I'm innocent and Deena Lewis is a manipulative bitch and a liar."

The detective's eyebrows weren't the only ones that went up.

Deena's screech echoed in the hallway. "You bastard!"

Wow. That worked better than he'd hoped.

The crowd parted as Deena shoved people out of the way.

The detective and his partner looked surprised and annoyed to see her there, but she didn't seem care. Her entire focus was on Garrick, her face red and eyes wild.

"You did this to me!" she yelled, pointing at her battered face.

Garrick winced. *God, that must hurt.* His stomach churned at the idea that even one of his teammates might believe he'd done that.

Deena stepped forward, boldly displaying the damage to everyone before turning back to Garrick. "You did this. You forced yourself on me. I said no! I said no at least five times!"

To Garrick, it sounded like she was reciting her prepared story, but he didn't trust that anyone else heard it that way.

There was no stopping Deena now that she'd warmed up to her audience. The drama went full tilt as she gasped and howled accusations. The crowd around her shifted with growing unease, her words echoing around them.

Garrick stood frozen, trapped in a nightmare and unable to wake up. The awkward stares, or worse, the men avoiding any eye contact, filled him with a potent mixture of sadness and rage. How could they possibly believe her? They *knew* him.

The only bright spot was the unexpected support from Tim, Dave, and Chris. They lined up, shoulder to shoulder with Mike and Alexei, forming a wall behind Deena, their expressions ranging from incredulous to disgusted.

Jack and Rupert moved to Garrick's sides.

The support was heartwarming. Too bad it wouldn't make one bit of difference.

Deena was going all out now, flailing her arms, and he flinched at the terrible things she claimed he'd done. He had no idea how to end this. He thought she might actually squeak out a tear, her next baleful cry of dismay over his cruelty still ringing in the air, when a deep voice boomed over all their heads.

"Enough!"

Everyone, even Deena, went silent.

Rhian plowed through the crowd. He looked as exhausted as Garrick felt. He also had a very big, very dark hickey on his neck.

Garrick tried not to cringe. He vaguely remembered latching onto that exact spot last night, but he hadn't realized what he'd done. And he would have felt bad about it but he was too busy staring daggers at Rhian. If Rhian had any capacity for reading his expression or his mind, he would understand the message loud and clear.

Don't. You. Fucking. Dare.

Deena's eyes narrowed on Rhian as he came to stand in the middle of their insane tableau, the hatred in her gaze unnerving.

The detective in charge looked Rhian over. "And you are?"

Rhian didn't hesitate.

"I'm his alibi."

Rhian stood calmly as forty or so pairs of eyes landed on him. Not on his face, which he kept bland. Not on his lips, which had just uttered potentially the most disastrous words he'd ever uttered. But on his neck and the glaringly obvious love-bite—the first of its kind to ever grace his person—emblazoned there.

Yep, this was going to be a real cluster fuck.

His entire life, from age six when his first foster family had put him on skates until now, had been focused on one thing. One goal. The NHL. And that goal was a mere twenty-four hours away from being a dream come true. But here, now, he was putting that and everything else he had on the line. A decision he was remarkably comfortable with, regardless of being scared witless.

He'd been shocked when Garrick had made him promise not to alibi him. Then pissed. Then, sitting in his apartment staring at that stupid TV, he'd been ashamed to feel relieved.

He could pull up stakes. Take off. Leave it all behind. No attachments. No things.

Garrick would understand. Hell, Garrick was insisting on it. And it was what he should do. What he should want to do.

Only, as he'd driven to Garrick's farmhouse, he'd known it was a lie. He'd never leave it all behind. There would always be this attachment, even when he was in another city, on another team, in another lover's arms—though the latter was impossible to imagine at this point. There was this *thing*. Love. And he finally understood what it meant. Love, in its simplest form, was what his mother had never been able to give him. What no family had ever found a way to offer.

Protection.

He had to protect Garrick.

It would help, Rhian thought with an inward sigh, if Garrick would stop glaring at him like he'd like to pound him into the floor.

As if reading his mind, Rupert squeezed Garrick's arm hard enough to turn Garrick's skin white.

Garrick aimed his glare at Rupert, and Rhian approached the detective. He smiled and held out his hand, wishing like hell he could do this in private.

"I'm Rhian Savage. Garrick told me what was happening yesterday when Deena approached the league about this." He hoped the cops also thought that was suspicious. "As I understand it, she's claiming Garrick assaulted her the night before last after he left Quigley's Bar and Grill. As the hostess, Sandy, can attest, as well as Rupert," he pointed at Rupert and carefully ignored Reese, who had faded into the background of the crowd, "I left within five minutes of Garrick. I went directly to his house and he was there when I arrived."

He ignored the wide-eyed looks being exchanged.

At least he had the detective's undivided attention. "And how long did you stay?"

In for a penny, in for a pound. "I spent the night."

193

Everyone went still. Rhian didn't dare glance at Garrick.

"Rhian is headed to the NHL," Garrick said with great pride, as if this explained his sleepover. "He had a bunch of shit on his mind, so he came over to talk it out in private."

Rhian nodded and followed Garrick's lead. "Yeah, been nervous about that and fortunately for Garrick, I invited myself over." The nervous part was total bullshit and a good number of the people present probably knew it. He and Garrick might be digging themselves into a hole, but he kept shoveling for all he was worth.

Now even the detective was staring at the fucking hickey. "Do you have any way of proving you were there?"

"I don't think so. I didn't make any calls or anything. It was late and we—" *went straight to bed after fucking on the dining room table.*

While he choked on the lie, Garrick jumped in. "We talked. We didn't go online or go anywhere. It was just us. Talking. Until late."

Good god, Garrick was the *worst* liar. He would single-handedly convince the entire team they'd fucked like crazed monkeys all night if he didn't shut up.

"Do you need a statement?" Rhian asked before Garrick could open his mouth again.

The detective nodded. "I'm going to need all of you who were at Quigley's that night to come with me." He turned to Deena. "And you should probably come along as well."

Deena's eyes widened. "Why do I have to go? I already told you what happened." She pointed at Rhian. "He's a liar!"

Steve stepped forward, his smile smug, a clear warning in his eyes.

"I'm not lying," Rhian said firmly. "She is."

"I'm not!"

"Deena, don't do this," Garrick pleaded.

"No, Garrick, *you* don't do this. I'm telling the truth."

Her shrill cry sounded particularly unconvincing. Then she turned all that crazy on Rhian and he almost stepped back to get away from the madness in her eyes.

"You should think about what telling the truth really means, Rhian."

Rhian shook his head. "No, Deena, you need to think about what your bullshit is doing. How can you live with yourself?"

Rhian knew he'd made a mistake as soon as the words left his mouth.

Chapter Twenty Five

Deena melted down before everyone's eyes, her focus fixed on Rhian. Garrick had wanted her to crack, to come completely unhinged in front of the cops, but not at Rhian. Garrick had to do something to get her attention back on him.

"Deena!"

She wasn't the only one who jumped when he hollered her name.

"Tell the truth, is all this because I wouldn't sleep with you?"

It was hard to say who was more stunned by his accusation. Maybe Rhian. Or the detective. Or Steve.

Or Deena. "*What*?"

"Look around you, Deena. Everyone here knows you've been trying to work your way through—or should I say under?—every man on the team."

Yup. Now Rhian definitely appeared the most shocked, though most of the men who knew him were agape. Garrick had never in his life spoken to a woman with such contempt and disrespect. He wanted to wash his own mouth out with soap. *Jesus.* If this backfired, he was making his situation worse. The risk was nauseating.

Deena forgot all about Rhian. She turned to Garrick and glared at him through narrow eyes. "Excuse me?"

"Oh, come on, Deena. You're the ultimate Puck Bunny, and I said no. For five seasons I've been telling you no." He turned to their audience as if to solicit support, though not able to actually make eye contact while this filth came from his mouth. "I wouldn't touch *that*," he said, pointing at Deena, "with a ten foot pole."

Deena growled a second before she launched into the air, her hands lashing at him.

"*You bastard,*" she shrieked.

He jumped back, hoping the cops would stop her before she removed his face with her claws. It was Alexei, though, who caught her with an arm across her chest. She flailed against him. Alexei barely winced as her heels struck his shins and lacquered talons tore at his shirt.

Alexei looked to Garrick, silently asking what he should do. Garrick didn't have the damndest idea. He did know that the expression on the detective's face proved it was working to his advantage for Deena to show her true colors. Her true *totally barking mad* colors.

He did the most infuriating thing he could think of—he smirked at Deena.

"I would never let you touch me," Deena screamed. "You're disgusting."

The way she said it unnerved Garrick. He wanted to lunge forward and clap a hand over her mouth, but he couldn't. He caught Rhian's frantic stare.

Garrick had a terrible feeling he'd overplayed his hand.

"You fucking faggot! It's not me. It's because I'm a woman! You're a fucking queer. You wouldn't know what to do with a woman if she was crazy enough to let you touch her in the first place. You're a fucking pervert!"

The color drain from Rhian's face.

Garrick focused on one thing—she hadn't said Rhian's name. Garrick could weather this, but *fuck*, he didn't know where to look. What to do.

Jack's hand on his arm brought him up short.

"Which is it?" Jack demanded.

Garrick looked at his friend, confused. Jack stared Deena down.

"Which is it?" he repeated.

"What?" Deena asked.

"Did he rape you or is he gay? Which is it?"

If Garrick hadn't been struck dumb by the fact that his sexuality was being discussed at very high volume in a public place, he might have kissed Jack, rumors be damned.

Deena appeared positively stumped.

The detective turned to her. "It's a good question, Ms. Lewis. As I understand it, gay men rarely rape women. And you indicated Mr. LeBlanc wouldn't know what to do with a woman, should he find himself with one."

A few snickers rippled through the crowd.

Deena hung from Alexei's arm. She turned to Steve. "What do I do?"

Garrick felt a surge of victory.

Then Steve stepped forward and pulled out his phone.

"I don't know anything about what this crazy bitch is talking about with the rape," he said calmly, ignoring Deena when she launched at him. Alexei held on, barely. "But I can confirm that Garrick LeBlanc is gay."

"You bastard! You fucking bastard," Deena screeched. "You were the one who told me to say he raped me. It was your idea!"

Garrick would have been gratified by this admission, but he couldn't tear his eyes from Steve's phone. Goddamn it, Steve held Rhian's entire future in the palm of his hand.

Deena lurched forward and Alexei staggered, letting Deena career into Steve. To anyone who didn't know Alexei well, it appeared he'd been forced off balance by Deena's struggles. In reality, it was an old trick Alexei liked to employ on the ice to effectively rearrange an opponent without incurring a penalty.

Alexei reeled Deena back in while Steve tried to get out of the way, steadied by a helpful hand. Tim's, if Garrick wasn't mistaken. Then Mike's arm snaked out from the crowd to flip the phone from Steve's fingers. Chris deftly grabbed it midair.

In a nanosecond, the phone disappeared into the knot of players at Steve's back.

Steve spun around. "Give me that!" he yelled.

Not one of Garrick's friends moved, except to hold out their perfectly empty hands and smile.

Chris was the picture of wide-eyed innocence. "Give you what?"

Garrick bit his lip to hide his smile and wondered if Steve would want his phone back if he learned it was now shoved into someone's sweaty jock strap.

Steve turned red. "My phone!"

Alexei, ever the keen strategist, chose that moment to release Deena. She fell on Steve like the proverbial woman scorned.

Steve howled and blood welled from the long scratches scoring his cheeks. In a flurry of limbs, he and Deena crashed to the concrete floor.

After a moment of stunned immobility, the cops jumped into the fray and pulled Deena and Steve apart with considerable effort. Garrick waited for them to demand the return of Steve's phone, but either they didn't give a shit or they were too preoccupied by Deena's caterwauling and Steve's loud protestations of innocence.

The important things were Deena's loud and repeated accusations that Steve had put her up to the rape charge, and the cops apologizing to Garrick for the misunderstanding.

As soon as the show was over, their audience dispersed. Garrick apologized to his teammates for the drama and what he'd said to incite Deena. He thanked his friends for their help, shocked when Tim put an arm around his shoulders, while Dave and Chris grinned.

"Man, you're just *full* of surprises, aren't you?" Dave crowed.

The guys laughed at the blush heating Garrick's face, leaving him with a few congratulatory whacks on the ass before going back into the gym. He smiled at their retreating backs. The weight pressing down on his chest since they'd left Quigley's two nights ago lifted.

Another screech from down the corridor brought his attention back to the police. He spoke briefly with the detective, asking if anything could be done to get Deena help. She wasn't innocent by a long shot, but she was also a victim in all this.

When at last the detective left, Garrick turned to follow Rupert to his office so he could quietly have a nervous breakdown. He'd made it only a few steps when Alexei caught his eye and nodded to the trainer's office.

Rhian stood with Mike in the empty office, trying not to fidget as they waited for Alexei and Garrick. Mike had yanked him in here while the cops had been handcuffing Steve, a spectacle Rhian had no desire to witness. He was relieved the entire ordeal was over, but ultimately, it was a sad end to a terrible situation.

Mike pulled Steve's phone from the back of his shorts. Rhian forgot how to breathe. Somewhere on that phone was proof of Garrick being gay. Of Rhian being gay. Sort of.

Should he launch into an explanation about labels and bisexuality? Probably not helpful at this point.

Alexei and Garrick entered the room and Alexei shut the door behind him. The second he held out his hand, Mike tossed him the phone and Rhian watched in wide-eyed horror as it sailed through the air.

Alexei caught it deftly and tapped the screen exactly three times before his eyebrows disappeared beneath his shaggy hair.

Rhian's heart fucking stopped. He jumped a foot when burst of laughter exploded from Alexei.

Rhian opened his mouth, not even sure what the fuck he could say. *It's not what you think. Oh wait, yes it is, but...*

Alexei grinned, dropped the phone to the floor and brought his heel down with a resounding crunch. Plastic shrapnel scattered in all directions. A second stomp annihilated what was left of the phone.

"That should take care of that," Alexei said with a nod.

Mike bent to pick up the SD card. "Come on, gather all the pieces."

They did, quickly, without asking questions. When the remains of the phone were piled in Mike's hand, he went to one of the trainer's bins of soapy water and dumped the detritus into the suds.

Mike brushed his hands off about the water. "*That* should take care of it. There's always a chance he backed the pictures up somewhere, but let's hope not."

Rhian stared at his friends, speechless.

Alexei shrugged. "From that angle, you see Garrick's face clear enough, but not Rhian."

Rhian's eyes went wide.

"You going to tell me it's not you?"

Rhian hesitated, then shook his head.

Alexei smiled. "Garrick here can take a hit. You? You don't need any bad publicity right now. It's good your face is not showing."

"Thanks," he choked out.

"You're welcome," Mike said as he moved to stand beside Alexei.

They exchanged a quiet, startlingly intimate look and threaded their fingers together.

Rhian stared at their joined hands.

"Oh," he said lamely, a smile tugging at his lips. "Oh!"

Garrick started to laugh.

Alexei grinned. "What? You think you're the only gay guys in hockey?"

Garrick laughed even harder.

"Come," Alexei said to Mike as he towed him toward the door. "I have a sudden craving for butter. Let's go home for lunch."

Garrick's laughter stopped abruptly, his face transformed

201

to dawning horror.

Alexei and Mike let go of each other's hands and stepped from the trainer's office, closing the door behind them.

Rhian's light mood died when Garrick turned to him with a dark look.

"You shouldn't have done that."

"It was the right thing to do." And he refused to apologize for it. He didn't much appreciate being yelled at for it, either.

"No, it wasn't. You need to think about yourself first. This is the big time. You have to stay away from me. The rumors are going to be rampant, and you went and fucking admitted to spending the night at my house. And that *hickey*. You should—"

Rhian pressed his mouth to Garrick's.

Garrick stood frozen, his eyes wide as Rhian gently rubbed one more kiss against his lips. "Thank you."

"For what?"

Rhian couldn't say. Wouldn't. He turned for the door. "Goodbye, Garrick."

"No, wait."

With all his heart, Rhian wanted to stay in this room with Garrick and never walk back out into the world. He'd gladly give up having to go clear out his locker with a huge hickey on his neck after having admitted to spending the night at Garrick's. Would be grateful not to have to lie about something he wasn't remotely ashamed of.

But he couldn't have what he wanted. Not any of it.

He smiled over his shoulder at Garrick. "I suggest you come clean. I know it was important that no one know about Savannah while she still worked here, but your friends should know the truth."

"But the truth—"

"The truth is that you're going to marry her someday. Have a pack of kids running around your farmhouse. Make a family."

Garrick didn't deny it, even nodding a little. He always

been honest with Rhian, and it was time for Rhian to be the same with himself.

Without another word, he walked away.

Chapter Twenty Six

Garrick spent the afternoon attempting to drink all his troubles away. It didn't work, but when Jack had suggested they go out for lunch and a beer to celebrate his narrow escape from Deena's insanity, he'd leaped at the distraction.

He'd asked Rick to pull him off the ice the day before. What had loomed as a "big moment" in his career was of surprisingly little impact when compared to the relief of Deena and Steve being carted away by the police and the agony of Rhian walking away.

What the fuck was up with that? It was best for Rhian to stay away from him until he left for Boston, but that goodbye had felt a whole lot more permanent than *I'll see you in the few months*.

But then it wasn't like they could go on as they had been. So really, once again, Rhian was doing what needed to be done. And Garrick was sitting here lamenting it for all he was worth.

"You going to sit there staring at that beer all afternoon or what?" Jack asked.

Garrick grunted. "Sorry. I'm not good company today."

"No shit, dude."

Garrick gave him the finger.

Jack laughed. "Listen, you want to tell me what the hell is going on?"

Garrick thought about playing dumb but couldn't bring himself to do it. He didn't want to lie. First of all, he sucked at it. And secondly, Jack was his oldest friend. If he couldn't cope with who Garrick was, then Garrick might as well know it up front.

"I'm bisexual," he stated baldly, watching Jack for his reaction.

Jack smiled. "Congratulations."

Garrick stared at him, *hard*, and waited for whatever came next. When Jack just took a sip of his beer and kept smiling, Garrick wanted to pop him one.

"That's all you're going to say? Congratulations?"

Jack laughed. "Yeah, that's about it. Do you want me to tell you I'm gay?"

"What? No. I mean, not if you aren't."

"What if I am?"

Garrick refused to be confused. "So what if you are? You want a membership pin or something?"

Jack rolled his eyes.

Garrick chuckled. "Fine, I see your point."

Jack grinned and slapped him on the shoulder. "You were expecting me to freak out, weren't you?"

"I was kind of hoping you wouldn't."

"Yeah, well, no worries there. I am, you know."

"You are what?"

Jack scanned the sparsely populated bar and shrugged, having apparently decided it didn't matter if they could hear or not. "Gay."

Garrick blinked at his friend. "Huh."

Jack smiled. "Is that all you're going to say?"

Garrick grinned. "Congratulations."

They both cracked up then sat quietly for a while, enjoying their beers and generally being better company than they had been. Eventually, Jack asked the question Garrick had been waiting for.

"Savannah know?"

"About being bi, or about Rhian?"

Jack's eyebrows shot up. "So the Rhian sleeping over thing wasn't a coincidence."

"It is as far as anyone else is concerned."

"Even Savannah?"

Garrick smiled. "No, not Savannah. She knows. Hell, it was her idea."

Another explanation of Savannah's wild idea and she had Jack firmly in her fan club.

"So, if she's cool with it, and you're cool with it, and everyone else is just speculating about it, why the hell have you been gazing into your beer all afternoon like it might hold the answers to the universe?"

Garrick sighed and met Jack's piercing blue eyes. "Rhian leaves for Boston tomorrow."

"And?"

"And nothing. We said goodbye. It's over." He shrugged, trying to convince himself as much as Jack that it wasn't a big deal.

He jumped when Jack's hand landed on his shoulder and held on, only then realizing he'd returned to brooding into his beer.

Jack called for another round plus a couple shots of whiskey. When the fresh drinks were delivered, Jack smiled grimly. "I figured we can sit here and drink ourselves into a stupor."

Garrick had no complaints with this plan, but he was curious. "Why would we do that?"

"It's the only cure I know for a broken heart."

Rhian stared at the entire contents of his life stacked in one corner of his ugly living room. Had it not been for the TV in its box, it would have fit in the miniscule front hall. Had it not been for the length of time it took to call Mike and give him his contact information in Boston, Rhian would have hit his ninety minute ready-to-go requirement, and not taken a whole hundred and two minutes instead.

He could draw it out further by calling a few other people, but ultimately, Mike and Alexei—and Garrick of course—were the ones he'd take with him when he left. At least with Mike and Alexei, he could reach out as soon as he got to Boston.

He wouldn't be able to do that with Garrick. Not for a while. He'd get over it eventually. In the meantime, being faced with Savannah every day would be an excellent reminder of why there was no place for Garrick in the next iteration of Rhian's life.

So this was it. A couple boxes, a couple suitcases, a hockey bag. All that there ever was and all that there ever would be.

He hoped someday he might find comfort in that again, but he suspected he'd gone and fucked it up. For almost twenty years he'd known and understood he wasn't someone other people kept. That hadn't changed. What *had* changed was that for the first time, he wished like hell things were different. For the first time in more years than he could remember, he wished that just this once, someone would fucking keep *him*.

He jumped when the doorbell rang, then went to greet the shipping company and help load everything into the truck. There was no point hiring a mover when he didn't have anything to move and no address to move it into. Hell, he'd even sold his car back to the dealership he'd purchased it from little more than a year before. A nice, clean exit.

He planned an equally simple arrival in Boston. He'd found an extended-stay hotel for the first couple months and would see where things went from there. In the meantime, the post office would hold his belongings until he claimed them in a few days.

Clean and simple. Just the way he liked it.

Right?

Garrick fell out of Jack's pick-up truck and barely avoided face-planting on the gravel. Jack laughed from behind the wheel, cheerfully sober and enjoying the show.

At some point, Garrick had realized Jack was pouring liquid medicine down his throat while only sipping his own drink. Garrick hadn't cared. If nothing else, he'd needed a sober ride home.

"I'll come get you in the morning," Jack said as he leaned over to slam the door shut. He idled in the driveway until Garrick made it into the house.

Wishing he could go straight to bed, Garrick did the right thing and detoured to the kitchen to get some water and ibuprofen. He was almost done chugging the second huge glass when his computer chimed in the corner.

He checked the time. One o'clock in the morning? That couldn't be good.

After almost missing the stool all together, he managed to plant his ass on the seat and hit the button.

Savannah's face popped up on the screen.

"What's wrong?"

Her smile faded. "What the hell happened to you?"

He looked down at himself and didn't see anything wrong. "What?"

"Are you drunk?"

He smiled. "Very."

She rolled her eyes. "Celebrating your near miss with the law?"

He fiddled with the mouse. "Yeah. Something like that."

When she cocked her head and studied him through his monitor, he tried to sit up a little taller.

"What are you doing up at this hour? Is everything okay?" he asked.

"Everything's fine. I just thought I would check in after my game. I got your texts while I was trapped in meetings and pre-game prep. I'm sorry I couldn't call."

"It's cool. I was out drinking with Jack most of the day anyway."

"I can see that," she said with a smirk. "How's Rhian?"

Garrick slumped. "I wouldn't know."

"He didn't go out with you tonight?"

"He had his last game... Oh shit. I missed it. Some friend I am."

"I'm sure he understands."

Garrick harrumphed. "I'm really sure he doesn't. I told him to stay away from me. Yelled at him for giving me an alibi."

Savannah grimaced. "Ouch."

"It seemed like the right thing to do at the time," he mumbled.

For a long time, she just stared at him. He tried to find comfort in those familiar smoky green eyes. He loved this woman with all his heart. Which was a funny thing, since it turned out all his heart had room for two.

"Savannah?"

"Yes, Garrick?"

"I love you."

"I know. And I love you. It's how I know you're going to do the right thing."

"And what's that?"

"I'm just as certain you know the answer to that."

"But—"

"Goodnight, Garrick."

In a blink, she was gone.

Chapter Twenty Seven

Garrick woke at dawn, certain of two things. One, he needed more painkillers. Two, he needed to get to the Moncton Airport. *Now.*

He called Jack to ask for a ride. Jack laughed. "Look out your window, asshole. Your truck is in the driveway."

Garrick did, and sure enough, it was. "How did you—"

"I figured once you sobered up and stopped feeling sorry for yourself, you might have somewhere to be."

Garrick grinned even though it hurt his face. "Jack, I fucking love you."

He chuckled. "That seems to be going around these days, huh?"

Garrick started to protest, but Jack cut him off.

"Good luck."

"Thanks."

Garrick was tearing out of his driveway before he'd even come up with a plan. All he was going on was *must see Rhian.*

Rhian staggered along the concourse of the Moncton Airport, numb with exhaustion. He'd sat up all night, alone on his couch, staring at the wall. His sheets were packed. The TV gone off to Boston. He'd had that new couch the landlord had delivered the week before and his thoughts for company, and that was it.

Neither had given him any comfort.

Restless, he checked the departures screen again. His flight wasn't boarding yet. Not that he wouldn't have heard the announcement over the PA system. The Moncton airport only had a handful of gates, so even now, when he was as far from his gate as he could get without leaving the building, he would have heard.

He needed to get on that plane and fly away. He was almost gone.

Turning, he paced once more past the café and bookstore, his face blank and his eyes down. He ignored the bite of his carry-on bag's strap on his shoulder and focused entirely on putting one foot in front of the other.

When he heard Garrick call his name, he thought he might actually be hallucinating.

He turned and blinked at the sight of Garrick running toward him. Hope flared, but Rhian squashed it ruthlessly.

Garrick skidded to a stop at his side. He looked at shitty as Rhian felt.

He strongly suspected he did not want to hear whatever had driven Garrick out of bed—given the wild case of bedhead he was sporting—and directly to the airport. When Garrick continued to do nothing more than stare at him, Rhian caved, deciding he'd rather just rip the Band-Aid off.

"What do you want?" His voice rasped like his throat was lined with sandpaper.

Garrick gazed down at Rhian's mouth like he wanted to attack him. In a good way. Which was *bad*.

Rhian would fucking punch the guy in the nose if he even tried it. This was hard enough.

Garrick grabbed Rhian's arm and dragged him to the bookstore. "Come here."

Rhian let himself be towed along.

They approached the register and Garrick turned on his mega-watt smile. "Lisa, could I borrow your stock room for a couple minutes?"

Lisa returned his smile and led the way to the steel door in the back corner. "Sure, Garrick."

Rhian resisted the urge to roll his eyes. Of course Garrick knew her. And she knew him. He knew everyone in this damn town.

As soon as the door closed behind them, Rhian stepped as far away from Garrick as he could, let his bag fall to the floor, and crossed his arms over his chest.

He waited for Garrick to say something. Rhian had nothing to add to their final goodbye.

Garrick's huge frame consumed the small space. Rhian was reminded of an elevator ride just a few short week ago. If he'd known then that they'd end up here, he might have done things differently.

No, that was bullshit. He wouldn't change a damn thing.

"Was it just sex?"

Rhian blinked. "What?"

"Was it just sex, Rhian? Just a fling?"

God, that was all it was *supposed* to have been. Rhian knew he should lie, but he couldn't. "No."

"You felt it too, didn't you?"

Rhian's heart kicked, but he tightened his arms across his chest and looked away. "Whatever."

Garrick shoved back into the door and Rhian threw his hands out to steady himself. Garrick smashed their chests together the minute his arms were out of the way, his nose almost bumping Rhian's.

"Tell me the truth, Rhian."

"What does it matter?" He turned his head and stared at Garrick's shoulder, not up into those soft brown eyes. "You have Savannah."

Just saying her name firmed his resolve.

"I do," Garrick agreed.

Rhian wondered if Garrick had come all the way to the airport just to make him feel like total crap.

"And she knows," Garrick finished.

"She knows what?"

"That I love you."

Rhian looked up, pinned under Garrick's direct gaze as

amber turned to chocolate and the earth tilted on its axis.

"What?" His lips formed the word but almost no sound came out.

"I love you."

Rhian shook his head. "No." He shook his head harder. Faster. "You can't love me."

"I do."

"But not like—"

"*Just like.* Just like I love Savannah. More than I've ever loved anyone else on earth but the two of you."

Rhian swallowed hard. "It's not possible."

Garrick's mouth kicked up on one side and he shrugged. "Two weeks ago I would have agreed. But then there was you. And I'm telling you it's not just possible, it's the truth."

Rhian didn't realize he was still shaking his head until Garrick's hand cupped his cheek and stilled the movement.

"I love you."

"Stop saying that."

"No."

Rhian stared at Garrick, mute, horrified to discover that knowing the man he loved, loved him in return, was actually worse than believing it couldn't possibly be the case. Because it didn't matter. Garrick could love Rhian as much as he wanted, claim to love him as much as anyone in the world, but in the end, Rhian knew the truth.

Garrick wouldn't *keep* him.

Garrick stared down at Rhian's stricken face. Grief unfurled in his belly. He'd done the unthinkable and declared his love, and poor Rhian looked terrified.

Hindsight was a *bitch*. He should have told Rhian somewhere else. Somewhere Garrick could lie on top of him until the raging anxiety ran its course and there was only the peaceful, easy Rhian who looked at Garrick with trust and—he hoped like hell—love.

But it was too late for that. He had to work with what he had, which was a storage closet and less than five minutes. Sliding his hands down Rhian's arms, he circled both wrists with his thumb and forefinger, then pressed his arms, torso, hips, and legs against Rhian's, pinning as much of his lover as he could against the door.

"Please say something," he murmured.

Rhian's panting breaths blew across his lips.

When Rhian shook his head, Garrick stopped him by pressing their foreheads together. He swallowed against the lump lodged in his throat and offered Rhian an out. "I'll understand if you don't feel the same way—"

Rhian's body jolted against his.

Garrick eased back. "I'm sorry. I'm being stupid. I can go—"

Rhian halted his awkward apology by tilting his head and bringing their mouths together. Calling it a kiss would have been generous, but hope surged through Garrick.

Rhian pulled his lips away before Garrick could do more than murmur his surprise.

"I'm scared."

The whispered admission tore at Garrick, the crack in Rhian's voice revealing how much the truth had cost him.

"I'm sorry. I didn't mean to frighten you."

Rhian didn't say anything.

Garrick sighed. "Would you like me to leave you alone?"

"No."

The immediate denial was some comfort, but Garrick thought he'd already pushed way past Rhian's limits.

"It's okay. Maybe you can think about it. If you, you know, want to be in touch, or we can talk sometime, maybe—"

"Garrick."

"Yes?"

"I love you."

Garrick slumped against Rhian. "Oh, thank Christ."

Rhian's voice was little more than a whisper in his ear. "I've never said that before. To anyone. Ever."

He released Rhian's wrists to wrap his arms around Rhian's rigid torso. What the fuck was wrong with people that a man as gentle and beautiful as this had been left alone his entire life?

Garrick pulled back to look into Rhian's wide cobalt eyes. "I promise you, Rhian, I will cherish it. Always."

"Really?"

Something about the disbelief on Rhian's face, the surprise in his voice, helped Garrick connect the dots. He wasn't angry or surprised Rhian doubted him, but didn't the stupid man realize what Garrick was telling him?

He was about to give him a detailed and thorough explanation, emphasized with long, hard kisses, when the faint sound of the public address system made its way through the heavy door.

"This is the last call for passenger Savage, on Air Canada flight 8937 to Toronto. Please check in at gate three immediately."

"Oh shit!" Rhian yelped.

Garrick jumped back. By the time the tinny voice was repeating the request, they were hauling ass through the bookstore and down the main concourse at full speed.

Rhian waved to the attendant at the gate as he staggered to a stop at the security checkpoint. He threw his bag onto the belt and turned to Garrick.

"So where do we go from here?"

Garrick laughed. "Boston."

Rhian grinned and ran to his gate.

About the Author

Samantha Wayland has always dreamed of being a novelist. She wrote her first book as an escape from the pressures of her day job. That fascinating piece of contemporary erotic mystery/suspense with elements of paranormal, international intrigue, and god only knows what else, is safely tucked under her bed, where it will remain until hell freezes over. Since then, she's learned a lot about the craft and turned her attention to writing contemporary MM and MMF ménage erotic romance.

Sam lives with her family—of both the two and four-legged variety—outside of Boston. She used to spend her days toiling away in corporate nerdville but was recently sprung from that hell. Now when she's not locked away in her home office, she can generally be found tucked in the corner of the local Thai place with a few beloved friends (and fellow authors).

Her favorite things include mango martinis, tiny Chihuahuas with big attitude problems, and the Oxford comma.

Sam loves to hear from readers.

Email her at samantha@samanthawayland.com, or find her on Facebook as Samantha Wayland and on Twitter as @SamWayland.

Also by Samantha Wayland

With Grace

A man yearning to explore his sexual tastes but afraid to turn up the heat, the woman who loves him but is hungry for more spice...and the chef who craves them both.

When Grace, Philip and Mark find a mobster's flash drive full of incriminating information, they are quickly embroiled in a dangerous situation. They stay together for safety, but proximity ignites the sparks they've long been fighting to ignore.

When three friends dare to succumb to their appetites, they find the perfect recipe for love.

Destiny Calls

Patrick didn't think it would be a big deal to kiss Brandon, his best friend and fellow police officer. Hell, they'd done crazier things to escape a bar fight. But then he had no way of knowing just how hot it would be.

Destiny Matthews is not a woman who is afraid to ask for what she wants, and when she sees her two best friends kissing, she knows just what she's going to ask for. Before she can convince Patrick that he's not as straight as he likes to protest, Brandon is attacked by an unknown enemy.

While they fight to protect each other's lives, they prove time and again that they're even better at protecting their own hearts.

Fair Play

Hat Trick Book One

Savannah Morrison is the new athletic trainer for the Moncton Ice Cats, a professional hockey team in the wilds of New Brunswick. It's a good thing she's got plenty of knowledge and grit, because as the only woman trainer in the league, she has to work twice as hard to win the players' respect. The last thing on earth she would do is date one of them.

Twelve year hockey veteran Garrick LeBlanc isn't ready to hang up his skates, particularly since he hasn't figured out what the hell he's planning to do next. He needs the new trainer to keep him fit to play, and she's got the skills to do it. Too bad he lost his mind and hit on her the day they met. Now she hates his guts and he's made an art of ignoring her.

When the team is put up for sale, Garrick and Savannah have to work together to save their jobs and their team. Somewhere along the way, they discover Garrick isn't just a hockey player, Savannah isn't only passionate about her work, and just maybe they've got more in common than they thought.

End Game

Hat Trick Book Three

Garrick LeBlanc never intended to fall in love with two people, but he has, and now he has to figure out what to do about it. He wants to make them happy, but is afraid he's doing just the opposite. To make matters worse, he's trapped in New Brunswick until the end of the hockey season, while his lovers are both in Boston.

Savannah Morrison has no one but herself to blame for practically shoving her lover into the arms of another man. After all, it was her idea that Garrick take a lover while they are separated for the season. She loves Garrick with all her heart, but how the hell is she going to share him with Rhian?

Rhian Savage used to have such a simple life. Now he's in love, his dreams of skating on an NHL team are coming true, and he keeps spotting a strangely familiar face in the crowds. To top it all off, he has to see Savannah every day. He knows she's Garrick's real future, but he doesn't have the balls to do the right thing for all of them and end it—until his life goes sideways. As usual.

Now Rhian is alone, Garrick is heartbroken, and Savannah—the one person Rhian figured would celebrate his departure—is beating down his door. What the hell is up with that?

28190752R00134

Made in the USA
Charleston, SC
04 April 2014